Teach Me

A Novel By

Amy Lynn Steele

For my high school sweetheart and the love of my life.

Thank you for being the magic in my world.

Dedicated to all those who know that love is a lesson learned.

Challenges make life interesting; however, overcoming them is what makes life meaningful.

Mark Twain

One

Allison

I didn't know it was possible, but falling for someone was easier than I expected. I have heard of summer love and all that—I mean who hasn't seen *Grease*?—but to experience it myself is a whole other story. He was right there in front of me, running with his surfboard into the waves. His sandy blonde hair flapped in the ocean breeze as his legs hit the first of the water, his skin tanned by hours under the California sun. I watched him, jaw open, as he made it look effortless.

I hadn't realized that I watched this stranger the entire time he was on his surfboard, but I did. When he exited the water, he glanced in my direction and smiled at me. I think I smiled back, but shock does funny things to a person's face. I watched every step he took as he made his way to a white truck in a nearby parking area. He put his surfboard in the bed and took out a towel. I watched as he dried off, his back to me. Suddenly, he turned around and caught me staring at him. I quickly lifted the book I had been reading to try to hide my face before Surfing Boy came splashing into view. Over the cover, I could see him smirk before he climbed into the cab of his truck.

It was impossible to focus on my book now. He was insanely cute, and he totally saw me checking him out. Oh well, it was a big beach, and the chances of seeing him again were slim to none. The next day, I went back to what I considered my usual spot, ready to focus on my book. I had been reading my way through some of the classics before I started my AP English class in the fall. I brought eight books with me, one to read each week of my vacation. At the time, I was reading Bram Stoker's *Dracula*. I wanted to forget about the really cute guy, and I thought a bloodsucking psychopath should do the trick. I opened my book to where I'd left off before the previous day's distraction.

Lucy was telling Mina how she had gone from no prospects of marriage to having three men to choose from. All three were great, but she loved one more than the other two. Lucy sent Mina word of her choice— the handsome and wealthy Lord Arthur Holmwood. If I had the choice, I would have picked Quincy Morris, the Texan cowboy. He may have been rough around the edges, but he was brave and had a heart the size of his home state. Yes, I would have picked Quincy, but unlike Lucy, I have no prospects.

My last boyfriend and I broke up before school ended. I knew he wasn't "the one," no matter how cute he was or how well we got along. Jeremy and I had dated exclusively during our junior year, and for the most part, it had been pretty fun. He was smart, funny, and everyone liked him. He had been more or less just a really good friend to me, and he wanted something more. Something I couldn't give him. I really wish I could have because he is a really great guy, just not my guy. He didn't understand why

2

we couldn't stay together, and I still hear from him once a week. My friends thought I was crazy, but when your heart talks, you have to listen.

I sat on a beautiful beach trying to forget a beautiful stranger. It's not easy since I had seen him the past four days in a row. Each day I sat there, trying to read my book, unable to focus on anything but *him*. He always smiled at me, and I just stared back. Just as the thought that I hadn't seen him crossed my mind, sand was kicked up into my face. I jumped to my feet and dropped my book.

"Sorry about that," a hidden voice said. I knew it was male, but his face was covered as he was pulling his shirt over his head. I was lost staring at his abs until his shirt was off. My eyes widened as I was now staring at Surfer Boy. He smiled at me, and my surroundings seemed to disappear. I stood mute, and he continued, "Sometimes the wind kicks up, and the sand will go where it will go." He said this simply as he dropped his shirt on top of his towel.

He didn't wait for me to respond, which was a good thing because I'm not sure I could have said anything even if I wanted to. I brushed the sand off myself and watched as he turned and made an easy jog to the water. Slowly I sank back onto my towel in a trance. From a distance, he was good-looking; up close, he was unreal. I shook my head, determined to focus on my reading. I don't remember how long I had been looking over the top of my book, watching him. It seemed I stared as long as he surfed because too soon he was emerging from the water and making his way back to his towel. At first he kept his eyes to the sand, then quickly glanced at me and smiled.

Crap. I almost smashed the thick book against my head. Close by I could hear muffled laugher. Great. Just freaking great. Maybe I should just introduce myself as the freakishly clumsy stalker. I am every man's dream woman, right? I sighed and kept the book so close to my face that I couldn't make out any of the words. A shadow stretched over me. I dared to look up and found him, cute Surfer Boy, standing over me. I stared at him over the rims of my sunglasses.

"Reading that way will strain your eyes," he commented. My tongue swelled and dried in my mouth. I don't know what expression my face wore, but it made him smile. He nodded and smiled even bigger. "I'm Cooper, by the way," he offered. My eyes widened as I took a sharp intake of breath. I couldn't speak, which is annoying because I am a fairly outgoing person. Cooper laughed into his hand, trying to hide it as a cough.

"Okay, Book Girl," he finally said after a few moments. "Well, just in case you decide you want to tell me your name or"—he looked down the beach, then back to me—"or speak at all," he added. "I surf this beach every day, just so you know."

Of course I know, Cooper, I have watched you for five days now. He smiled at me again, and my mind went blank.

"Well then," he said as he gathered his things and turned to leave, "I hope to see you tomorrow." With this, he turned and made his way to his truck. I watched him put his surfboard in the bed and climbed into the cab. He rolled down the windows to let the heat out. I took a few quick steps toward the parking area. Cooper was backing out, so I needed to steady my nerves. I only had this one chance to make a better first impression.

"Ali!" I yelled as he drove past. Cooper tapped the brakes of his truck and then suddenly pulled into an open parking spot. He leaned out the window and looked at me, almost quizzically. I cleared my throat. "My name," I said loudly. "It's Ali. Or uh . . . Allison."

The truck door opened, and Cooper got out. He ran his hand through his salt-matted hair and took a few steps toward me. I took inventory of him as he moved closer. He was tall, at least six feet. He has a swimmer's build, defined muscles hidden behind a scrawny frame. His hair looked browner at the roots, the top bleached by the sun. His eyes were light blue and crystal clear. It was like the summer sky had found its inspiration in this boy's eyes. I couldn't look away from his gaze.

"Allison," he said an arm's length away. I nodded woodenly.

"Or Ali," I repeated, feeling a slight blush rise to my face. "That's what my friends call me." Cooper nodded and studied me.

"Ali is easier to say than Book Girl." He shrugged and moved closer. The thrill of hearing him speak to me and move closer was like nothing I have ever felt before.

"Book Girl does have a charm to it," I commented. Cooper laughed, and I felt more relaxed.

"You're not from around here, are you?"

"Am I that obvious?"

"You are *that* obvious," Cooper said with double meaning, and the relaxed feeling was gone.

"I better get going," I said quickly and turned to gather my things. *I am stupid*, I decided. *So obviously stupid!* I rushed to jam all my beach things into my bag. I noticed a second pair of hands next to mine, and I glanced up to find Cooper squatting next to me. He picked up my copy of *Dracula* and ran his finger over the spine of the book.

"This is a great book," he said quietly. I stopped what I was doing and turned to look him. "I get *Dracula*, you know? Why he does what he does." I shook my head. *No, he sucks blood from people.*

"I haven't finished it yet." *Because I've been too distracted watching the way your body works in the waves.* He handed it back to me, and our fingers brushed together. The book tumbled softly to the sand, and we both moved forward to pick it up. Naturally, our heads collided. I started to fall backward, and Cooper grabbed my arm, pulling me level. Once I was stable and able to take in my surroundings, our faces were just inches apart.

"Ow," I mumbled and took a much-needed breath.

"Sorry about that," Cooper said and leaned a few inches back. But he doesn't look sorry. He looks as dazed as I felt.

I ran my fingers over my forehead, saying, "I'm all right." Not that he asked, but I needed to break away from his scrutinizing stare.

"Let me know when you do finish it," he said. "I would love to know what you think about it." I could smell the salt water on his skin, and I closed my eyes and took in a deep breath. A moment later, he released my hands and took a step back.

"I will finish it by tomorrow," I blurted out. Cooper's eyes widened.

"You still have, what, about three hundred pages left?" I shrugged and put the book in my bag and started backing away. Cooper took a step toward me and, in the process, stole the oxygen from my lungs.

"I'm a fast reader," I tell him. "And I only have about *two hundred* pages left." He arched an eyebrow. "Mina and Van Helsing are corresponding regarding Jonathan's diary." Cooper smiled and nodded. I found myself wondering if he had actually read the classic.

"You are halfway through," he agreed. "Will I see you here tomorrow?"

I smiled. "I sure hope so," I laughed and quickly turned to make my way down the path that led to my aunt's house. I could feel Cooper's incredible eyes follow me as I left.

As soon as I got home, I opened my book and got to work. Now I had to finish by tomorrow. I don't know why I felt like I had something to prove to Cooper. Maybe because I had been checking him out for the past five days, and I wanted him to think I was more than a beach bunny. I had been reading for about an hour when my aunt came home.

"Ali!" she called from downstairs. I closed my book and made my way down to find her.

"Hey, Aunt Trudy," I answered as I entered the kitchen. My aunt was a bit eccentric. She never married or had any children of her own, but she told me she didn't want it any other way. She is outgoing and full of life. I stay with her every summer for at least a month, but this year, we decided on two months as one last hurrah before my senior year. Trudy is my father's sister, and I have stayed with her every summer for the past ten years. A summer for every year my mom has been gone (it gives my dad a break).

"What would you like for dinner tonight?" she asked as she pulled her graying hair back into a loose ponytail. Aunt Trudy was not comfortable in a kitchen and mostly used hers to display her art. During the summers, I would spoil her with home-cooked meals a couple of times a week.

"Do you want me to make something?" I opened the refrigerator to see what I could whip up. She started shaking her head.

"No." She spun around. "Let's go out tonight." I smiled at her. I wondered why she would ask me if she already knew what she wanted to do. Maybe it is out of courtesy or just because of all those years she had been on her own. I agreed and went back to my room to freshen up. I looked at *Dracula* and decided that I would stay up all night to finish it if I had to. Ten minutes later, we were out the door and on our way to Aunt Trudy's favorite Mexican food restaurant. We hadn't eaten there that summer, but I had eaten there many times before. The hostess recognized my aunt and took us to a table in the center of the restaurant, where she liked to sit.

"I bet if you order a margarita, they'd bring you one," my aunt said.

"I'm not twenty-one yet, Aunt Trudy," I reminded her. "But I am almost eighteen."

"Come on," she encouraged me. "Let's try." Typical Aunt Trudy— life is just one big game. The waiter came up from behind me.

"Hey, Trudy," he said, "would you like your usual margarita?" Trudy laughed and nodded her head.

"Well, yes, I would, Ryan," she answered. "And one for my niece." She waved her hand toward me. "She is visiting me for the summer." I could feel the waiter shift to get a better look at me. I didn't even have my driver's license with me, not that it would've mattered since I was underage. I was immediately nervous and locked my gaze on to the table. I felt Aunt Trudy kick me in the leg.

"Ow!" I jerked my head up to scowl at her. She winked at me and then nodded toward the waiter. I reluctantly looked back, and my heart stopped in my chest.

It was Cooper from the beach.

"Well, Book Girl." He smiled. "How are you going to get all that reading done if you are out partying with Trudy here?" I opened my mouth and closed it again. *Focus, Ali*, I told myself, *don't act like an idiot.*

"I will finish it tonight, so no margarita for me. Thank you, Cooper," I said a little curter than I had intended. "Or is it Ryan?" *Maybe he uses a different name for the girls he meets. Typical surfer boy. And here I am, thinking he is all smart and different from other guys. I must be so naive.*

"Have you two met?" Aunt Trudy asked, obviously overcome with excitement. Cooper never took his eyes off me as he squatted down next to our table.

"Yes, we have, except he told me his name was Cooper," I told my aunt with unexpected anger and tore my gaze from his. Aunt Trudy started laughing. I don't know why I felt so frustrated. It's not like I even knew this guy or if I would see him again.

"It is, sweetheart," she laughed. "His name is Cooper Ryan, but I just call him Ryan." She touched my hand. I sat on the hard wooden chair and felt about two inches tall. Cooper laughed along with my aunt.

"I had the pleasure to meet Allison earlier today at the beach," Cooper Ryan answered. "And I hope to see her again tomorrow." This time his voice was lower, and he moved a little closer to me.

"Well, I need to use the ladies' room," Aunt Trudy announced, leaving us alone. I forced my eyes to break away from Aunt Trudy's empty chair back to Cooper, who was still kneeling next to me. My nerves bubbled from the excitement of him being so intimately close.

"So Trudy is your aunt?" he asked as he moved to the now-empty chair. I nodded as I watched him. The dim lighting of the restaurant made him even more handsome, if that were possible.

"I visit her every summer," I told him. "I'll be here until the end of August, before school starts in the fall."

Cooper's smile made his eyes sparkle. "Will you be at the beach tomorrow?" He looked so excited. His gaze made me feel beautiful, like he was an artist seeing the *Mona Lisa*. I didn't know why I felt this way. I was no beauty queen. But I couldn't help feeling like one when he was looking at me like that. For all he knew, I could be as crazy as my aunt.

"If I can get my reading done," I said. Without another word, he slipped out of the chair and held it out so Aunt Trudy could sit back down. He informed us that he would be right back with our drinks.

"Oh, Allison," Trudy said, "I have always liked Ryan. He is such a polite young man. And smart too." I nodded, just listening and trying to act like I wasn't interested. But of course I was. "And he graduated from San Diego State this past spring." *That* got my attention.

"He is out of college already?" I stammered.

Aunt Trudy smiled and nodded. "Yes, he was on an accelerated program and was able to put four years into about two and a half. I think he is somewhere in his twenties, maybe just twenty-one." I sighed. I was only seventeen. No way would he go for someone four years younger, even if I did turn eighteen in a few months.

"Here you go, ladies." Cooper was back with our drinks—a margarita for Aunt Trudy and a blended concoction for me. Dinner was good, and Cooper kept coming over to our table. The more he did, the more nervous I became. He just seemed so great in so many different ways; the last thing I wanted to do was to get my hopes up.

Back at home, I grabbed my book and got settled into bed. I had a long night of reading ahead of me. I fell asleep with visions of Count Dracula and Cooper all mixed up and distorted. Truth be told, it was mostly just of Cooper and how he looked on his surfboard, floating over the waves with the sun shimmering off the water that clung to his body.

Two

Cooper

After I spoke to Trudy when Ali was in the ladies' room, I knew what I had to do. Knowing that Allison would be back on the beach the following day, I asked Trudy's permission to take her niece out for dinner. I decided not to surf that day. I was nervous about asking her out and didn't want to smell like the ocean. Trudy told me that she was almost eighteen, which makes her just about three years younger, but like any guy, I still feared rejection. I pulled my truck into an empty spot in the small lot and spotted Allison immediately. I sat and watched her before I got out.

She kept looking down at her book, then would slowly scan the water. Was she looking for me? That got me moving. I came up from behind her. She wasn't reading *Dracula*; she must have finished it like she said she would. She was holding *Pride and Prejudice*. I guess she didn't do things halfway.

"That Mrs. Bennett will get on your nerves sooner or later," I finally said.

Allison slammed her book close and jumped as I bent down next to her. She looked so beautiful. She reminded me of Snow White. Her skin was as flawless as porcelain framed with dark, almost-black hair. Allison's big brown eyes were wide with surprise as she turned around to look at me. I took my sunglasses off and shifted my weight to kneel in the sand.

"I finished *Dracula* just like I said I would," she said quickly. Her warm breath touched my face, and I realized the close proximity of our lips. I blinked a couple of times, trying to form my next thought.

"And what did you think?" I asked, moving to sit beside her on the beach blanket. I hoped she wasn't upset at how I kept moving closer and closer—I couldn't seem to help myself.

Allison swallowed before she answered. "I liked it better than the movie." She shrugged but didn't move away

"Good," I laughed, "now I can go on respecting you." *Stupid! She just finished one of your favorite books, and you insult her. Real smooth.*

Ali let out a hard laugh. "Well, I'm so glad I can meet your expectations," she said defiantly and crossed her arms over her chest—the universal symbol of personal closure. Instinctively, I reached and touched her arm lightly. I had to ignore how soft her skin was and apologize.

"Now don't get me wrong, Ali. It's just that I find people usually cop out and don't finish the book if they can just watch the movie." My fingers made a path down her arm to the hand that was holding her forearm in hopes that she'll look at me. "All I'm saying is that I am impressed." Our fingers were now touching, and I was having a hard time focusing. "I mean you read, what, like 250 pages just last night alone. That is persistence." My fingers lingered over her hand, and I found myself taking note of the contrast of our skin. I was spending too much time under the sun.

"I am a fast reader," she mumbled, and I realized she was staring at my mouth, "and persistent." I looked from our hands to her mouth. Allison's lips were the color of pale coral petals and parted slightly when she realized I was staring at her. I needed to stay focused.

"Very impressive," I added, hoping she knew I was talking about the reading and not her lips. Okay, a little about her lips too.

I forced myself to lean back when what I really wanted to do was hold her soft cheek in my hand and press my lips to hers. My hand was still on Ali's, and she didn't seem to mind. All I could concentrate on was our touch. It felt comfortable and easy, like it was the most natural thing in the world. I looked up from our hands to find her staring at me. A short second later, I leaned back. I couldn't focus while I was so close to her. I shook my head, and my thoughts slowly came back to the reason I was there.

"No surfing today?" she asked, breaking the silence. I looked to the ocean, then back to her.

"Waves are crappy today," I said out loud. *And I have to work, then take you out on a date*, I added in my mind. When I spoke again, I lowered my voice, and she leaned toward me. "And I was hoping to do something different today."

Allison arched a dark eyebrow. "And what would that be?" I could feel my face get hot, embarrassed. I bent down to her eye level again. *Just say it,* I commanded myself.

"Allison, will you go out with me tonight?" I spoke so quickly I almost didn't understand what I said.

"You want to go out with me?" she asked, her voice sounding shocked. Both of her dark eyebrows arched on her forehead.

Oh. Crap. How arrogant am I? Allison must have a boyfriend. Wouldn't Trudy have told me? Maybe he is a tool, and she wants me to swoop in and sweep Ali off her feet. Play it cool. I can sweep.

I forced out a hard laugh. "Of course I do," I said, taking her hand easily. "I have never surfed a beach so many days in a row, but after seeing you that first day, I had to keep coming back." I had laid it all out on the line. Silence.

Allison's dark brown eyes rounded in surprise. She broke eye contact with me and looked down at my hand on top of hers. I thought she was going to shake my hand off, but instead, she laced the tips of our fingers together. My heartbeat quickened.

"So," she said, her voice low, "a date?" Her hand was warm around mine, and I couldn't help but move my thumb back and forth over her soft skin.

"How about I pick you up at your aunt Trudy's at six?" Her cheeks flushed, and she looked even more beautiful.

"Okay," Ali whispered. I moved closer to speak directly into her ear. She smelled like coconut and citrus.

"I don't think you know how adorable you are when you get embarrassed," I whispered. I didn't move: I was stuck in a limbo under her trance. "See you at six sharp." I stood quickly and left before I could say anything else or act on my impulses.

Work was a blur. I remember telling Sean, my best friend, about Allison. I am pretty sure that's all I could talk about. He remembered her from the night before and had pretty much stalked her from the shadows. At one point, he had threatened to ask her out if I didn't. I thought I might be annoying him with how much I was talking about her, but I didn't care.

"So," Sean said. I turned toward him as he continued, "You going to bring this Book Girl to the bonfire tonight?" *Dang it. I forgot all about that.*

"I don't know . . ." I let my sentence trail off. Sean knew me well.

"You forgot," he accused. *No, I just didn't remember.*

"I just don't think that is a first date kind of—"

"No way," Sean cut me off. "You will be there. It's our traditional end-of-the-year party, our last one." He was right.

Since we were in grade school, we always celebrated the summer with a bonfire—a way to welcome the carefree months of surf and sun. First it was with our families, then extended to our friends, and now it was just a huge group of people. With me going through college at an accelerated rate, this would probably be our last bash together. Sean still had two years left in college, and I'd been applying for jobs all over California, so who knows where I would end up?

"I'll see what I can do," I promised. Sean didn't look happy but knew me well enough to know that trying to change my mind was useless. I didn't care about the bonfire tonight. I had a date with Allison.

***

Before I left the house, my mother gave me some sound advice: take Trudy some flowers; it would win me some points. My mom is always saying stuff like that, teaching me the finer points on how to treat women. So on my way home, I stopped at the farmer's market and picked up a bouquet of wildflowers for Trudy and a single sunflower for Allison. They seemed fitting for both women.

When I got there, I stood at the door, waiting to knock. It was two minutes to six. I could hear them inside giggling, but it sounded like it was mostly Trudy. I was excited and nervous. I shifted the flowers to one hand and knocked. The laughing stopped, and a moment later, Trudy opened the door with a huge smile.

"Good evening, Trudy," I said, holding the wild bouquet toward her. "These are for you." I smiled as Trudy's mouth formed an O, and she took them from me.

"Ryan," she cooed, "you are such a charmer." She stepped back and waved an arm in. "Come in, please." I did. Trudy's place was what I would call "eclectic," but I didn't care about her paintings and furniture. I scanned the room for Allison. Just as I was thinking her name, she appeared from the kitchen.

Time stopped. She was the most beautiful person I had ever seen. She was wearing a long flowing white skirt and a pale yellow tank top; her dark hair was pulled up high. I wanted to drop the flower I was holding and run my fingers over her skin, from the base of her neck down to her shoulder.

"I'll just put these in some water," Trudy said, breaking my Allison trance. I noticed she was blushing at my stare and took a few steps toward me. I closed the distance between us and extended the sunflower to her.

"This made me think of you," I said quietly. Ali reached for it, and our fingers brushed again. It felt differently than it had earlier that day. It was more powerful, like it was backed with electricity. Our gazes met, and I knew we both felt it.

"It is beautiful," she said. "Thank you." I smiled at how something so simple could make her happy.

"Of course," I answered. Trudy came back into the room, and I took an unwilling step back. She had a sprig of what looked like lavender in her hand. She made her way to Ali and said something quietly to her, which made her blush. Ali shifted, and Trudy began to weave the lavender into Allison's dark hair. When she was done and Ali wasn't looking, she winked at me.

"Let me put that gorgeous sunflower into a big vase for you, Ali," Trudy said and took it from her. "Now get going, you two. The night is young, and so are you." And with that, we were on our date.

The night air was warm as the sun hung lazily in the sky. I wanted to hold Ali's hand as we walked to the truck but decided I didn't want to push it. I opened the door for her and helped her into the cab. Once I was inside, I turned to look at her. The setting sun made her look radiant. She glanced at me from the corner of her eye and then turned to face me. She looked down at her skirt, then touched her thin top.

"What is it?" she asked, alarmed. I reached out and took her hand, not caring if it seemed forward.

"You are stunning," I told her. We just stared at each other, and I felt gravity pulling me closer to her.

"You don't look too shabby yourself," she said back with a smile. I had to laugh at her assessment. I like a girl with a quick wit.

"I was going to wear board shorts and style my hair with surfboard wax. But then I thought, nah, I'd fancy it up for you." Ali started laughing, and I was lost in the sound of it. I cranked the engine and pulled away from the curb, not releasing her hand, letting them rest on the seat between us.

"So," she said after a few minutes of comfortable silence, "where are we going?"

"I hope you like Italian." I smiled. I was taking her to this little place that few people knew about. They served the best meatballs and garlic bread.

"Who doesn't?" she answered with a grin.

I liked her. "I think we are going to get along just fine." And I was right.

Dinner was great. No, "great" doesn't seem to describe it. We just clicked. We ate, talked, and laughed for almost three hours. We discussed our likes and dislikes, our goals and dreams, family and futures. We had so much in common that it was unreal, almost serendipitous. The more we talked, the more I felt connected with her. Ali loved books and English as much as I did, and she wanted to be a professor or a writer. She wasn't only incredibly beautiful—she was incredibly smart as well. I reached across the table and took her hand in mine. As I did this, she moved closer to me in the round booth. Once again, I wanted to take her delicate face in my hands and press my lips to hers. I leaned toward her.

"Hey, Coop," an irritatingly familiar voice said from behind me. Allison looked past me, and I turned to see Sean. He looked back and forth between us. "So are you going to introduce me?" I wanted to say, *"No, I'm not going to introduce you. I'm going to kill you."*

I cleared my throat. "Hey, Sean." I turned to face Ali, her cheeks adorably pink, and squeezed her fingers. "Allison, this is Sean—Sean, this is—"

"Book Girl," he cut me off, smiling. Ali's eyes grew, and then she nodded and smiled, looking at Sean.

"Hello, Sean," she started. "You are the guy who was at the restaurant last night, hiding in the shadows, right?" She pointed her finger at him and tipped her head to the side. Our jaws dropped open, and then Sean and I laughed. "Well, I'll let you boys chat, and I'll just . . . you know." Then she scooted out of the booth.

Sean turned to face me. "I think I'm in love," he said dreamily as he dropped into the booth, and I mock punched his arm.

"What are you doing here?" I was annoyed. He knew about this date. He shrugged and picked up a breadstick and took a bite.

"I'm not letting you get out of the bonfire, my friend." He chewed with his mouth open. "You need to be there. Bring Book Girl . . . Ali," he said, shrugging.

"Come on, Sean, this is our first date," I pleaded, willing him to understand.

"Dude, I said to bring her." He looked at me, frustrated for not getting what I was saying. "She is so hot, man. If you don't ask her, maybe I—" I didn't let him finish. I smacked the back of his head.

"Ask me what?" Ali asked as she slid in easily next to me.

"There is this bonfire tonight," I said quietly, turning to face her and block Sean's view. I hadn't realized how close she was and became immediately distracted by her petal-soft lips.

"It's tradition," Sean interrupted, but it didn't make us break eye contact.

Ali blinked and smiled, glancing quickly down toward my lips, then back up to meet my eyes. "Do you want to go to the bonfire?"

"I . . ." I didn't know what to say. I couldn't focus on anything. Ali smiled and winked.

"I guess we will see you later, Sean," she said past me. "It was nice meeting you." She turned back to me. I don't know how long we sat there, but at some point, Sean left.

"I don't think I have ever seen anyone silence Sean—ever," I told her, impressed. She bit her lip and looked down.

"So your friends call you Coop, huh?" she asked with a smile.

Three

Allison

"I don't want you to feel like you have to go to this bonfire," Cooper told me when we got back into his truck. At this point, I would have gone anywhere with him.

"Your friend said it was tradition." I shrugged. "And traditions shouldn't be broken." I felt nervous, but conflicted. It was peaceful being with Cooper. He turned toward me as we approached the stoplight and studied my face for a moment.

"We won't stay long, I promise," he told me quietly, looking like he was lost in a different thought. I smiled at him. The air had gone cold with the setting sun, and I rubbed my arms to warm myself. Cooper parked and turned to look for something behind the seat. A minute later, he held out a sweatshirt for me.

"Thank you," I said, taking it from him. I was thankful that in the darkness, he couldn't see the blush of my cheeks.

"Hey," Cooper said, reaching across the seat and taking my hand in his. "Don't be nervous," he said as he squeezed my fingers. "I won't leave your side." I smiled faintly at his reassurance. He turned to face me, his expression a cross between serious and nervous.

"Are you okay?" I asked, covering his hand with my free hand. He nodded slowly but didn't speak for what seemed like a full minute. My heart and head went into overdrive, trying to process what he could possibly be thinking.

"You are making me nervous," I finally blurted out.

"That is not my intention," he said. "I was just thinking how surreal all this is." He shifted and was now literally sitting on the edge of his seat. "I mean, when I first saw you on the beach, my initial thought was how cute you were." I had to look down as he said this. "And then the more I saw you, the more I had to know you. It was little things like how you would sit in the shade at the beach or the way you'd hold your bottle of water and try to balance your book." His voice dropped. "Then when you finally spoke to me, I knew I would just need more, and then tonight . . ." I looked back up to him as his voice trailed off.

"Tonight was surreal," I offered. Cooper let out a short laugh.

"To say the least." His free hand moved to my face, and my vision blurred. Coop's thumb traced my cheek, and my breath caught in my throat. "I don't know about you, but I have never been this comfortable with another person, let alone on a first date." His hand was warm on my skin, and I tried to regulate my heart rate so I could speak.

"I know what you mean," I said slowly. Not that I'd had a lot of dating experience, but I knew that I had never had this much fun with anyone before or felt this comfortable. It did feel incredibly natural. I wanted to tell him this, but instead, all that came out of my mouth was, "Natural."

"Exactly," he agreed, moving closer. I could almost feel his lips on mine. I had never wanted anything more.

Suddenly, the truck started shaking, and we both jumped back. *Earthquake*, was my first thought. I didn't understand that the shaking was linked with the loud shouts outside the cab. A couple of guys were rocking the truck back and forth and calling Cooper's name. They hadn't realized someone else was inside the truck with him until my back pressed against the passenger side window.

Cooper sighed. "Sorry about them," he said, sounding frustrated and a little embarrassed. "We don't have to do this," he added, almost hopefully. He nodded toward the beach, and I looked over his shoulder. I was surprised to see forty to fifty people around a huge fire.

I swallowed and smiled as best I could. "Come on, Sean said it was tradition." Cooper smiled, and my heart melted. *I can do this.*

We sat quietly in the cab of the truck for just another minute before we got out. Cooper took my hand back in his and pressed his lips very quickly to it. This replaced the intimate moment we lost to the rowdy boys.

"You ready for this?" he asked. I didn't answer. Instead, I just smiled and opened the door of the truck. I silently told myself, *Be brave and act confident.* Cooper came around the truck and slipped his hand back into mine.

This was one serious bonfire. The blaze of flames jumped ten feet into the sky throughout the night. Sean seemed stunned when he saw us arrive. He took it upon himself to lead me around and introduce me to as many people as he could. Even though people kept coming up to Cooper, he stayed close to me throughout the introductions. At one point, Sean looped his arm around me.

"Sean," Coop said, his voice sharp. Sean put his hands up in a surrender position and smiled crookedly. I reached until I found Cooper's hand and held it tightly in mine; our fingers laced together. The rest of the night, I was more than content to stay close to Cooper. Occasionally, he would slip his arm around my waist. It was like a fairy tale.

I ended up having fun, and toward the end of the night, most people just called me Coop's girl or Lady Coop. At first I tried to remind them of my name, but eventually, I gave up. I was wearing his SDSU hoodie, which made me look like his girlfriend, so I just went with it. Honestly, it gave me a secret high at the thought.

It was about eleven, and the party was still in full swing. One good thing about my aunt Trudy was that she tried to keep up with technology, unlike my dad. I sent her a text telling her where I was and what I was doing, and she replied telling me to have fun and to remember to lock the door when I got home. It was as easy as that. Trudy understood what it meant to be young, and she trusted Cooper Ryan.

I pulled Cooper's sweatshirt tighter around my body, trying to block out some of the ocean breeze. He noticed what I was doing and put his arm over my shoulder and pulled me close to his body. Wow. Just wow.

"I have a blanket in the truck. Stay right here, and I'll go grab it." He made a quick dash toward his truck. I stood alone and watched the party. Most of the people were way past drunk. Cooper and I had discovered that neither one of us cared for dinking because it made you do stupid things, and some of these people were proving our point. I turned around and started to slowly walk toward the water, away from the noisy drunk people. I hadn't walked too far before the voices seemed to fade.

What an interesting night, I thought. I never imagined I could feel so good with someone, especially so quickly. I knew Cooper was trying to get a job teaching and could end up anywhere, but I didn't want to think about that. I just wanted to focus on the *now*—to live in the moment. I heard soft footsteps from behind me.

"I wasn't gone long, and you're already sneaking off," Cooper said as he came up from behind me. "If you're looking for Sean, he isn't out here." I turned around and let out a hearty laugh, and Cooper joined me. He came closer and wrapped the blanket around my shoulders, holding the corners. He hesitated for a moment, then used them like reins and pulled me closer. I looked up and met his intense gaze.

It was like a dream. The waves crashing in the background paired with distant music, the fire giving off an orange glow that cast our faces into shadow. Even the stars overhead were twinkling through the coastal haze.

Cooper took both blanket corners into one hand and pulled me flat against his chest. With his free hand, he placed it under my already-elevated chin. His thumb traced my cheekbone, then over my bottom lip. My mouth parted under his touch. We both stood motionless, memorizing this moment. I let my eyes slowly close, and as I did this, Cooper's soft lips pressed into mine.

We just stood there, not moving—not even breathing. Then the sensation of his lips to mine kicked in, double time. Every nerve in my body came alive. It felt like my body was awakening for the first time, feeling then how it should always feel. Everything felt new, and it felt good. I eased my arms around his neck and pulled myself as close as I could. Cooper let the hand under my chin glide to the back of my head and knotted it into my hair while his other hand released the blanket and held the small of my back.

I was hyperaware of him. The scent of suntan lotion on his skin, the dark blue flecks of sapphire in his honest eyes, how his almost-blonde hair fell across his forehead. How long Coop's fingers were as he softly touched the exposed skin of my back. He tasted like peppermint and summer, and I wanted more. When his tongue brushed against my lips, my mouth slowly opened.

World War III could have started, and neither of us would have noticed. The entire world as we knew it was gone. That kiss changed everything. I knew right then and there that I was no longer the girl I had been three minutes earlier—I was different now. I didn't know what it was or how I knew, but I did. It was effortless to be with Cooper. I had been drowning, and he was not only my life vest, but also my oxygen.

The strange thing was that I never realized these things were missing. I didn't know that another person could fill these unknown voids, but he had. Without knowing it, Cooper was healing me, making me whole. I was no longer empty or lost. In one night, in one kiss, I felt it happen.

I fell head over heels—no turning back—in love with Cooper Ryan.

***

I will always look back on the weeks that followed that world-changing kiss as some of the best of my life. Cooper and I were inseparable. He still had to work most days, but only for a few hours. The rest of his time became our time. We would talk for hours about all kinds of things, and the more we discovered about each other, the more we fell into an unspoken love. I wanted to tell him how I felt, that I was falling in love with him, but the fear of rejection was much more powerful.

Cooper told me about his accelerated program and how it felt to graduate so much earlier than his friends. He confessed his love for books, all books. I told him how I have been the English tutor at Chino Preparatory Charter School for the past three years. This impressed him, but I told him I thought it made me a huge nerd.

"Well, from one nerd to another . . . I think a smart girl is sexy." My cheeks burned as I pressed my lips to his. During some of this time, we would just lie on the beach and read. I never knew being with someone could feel this good. Cooper told me he had a hard time meeting new people because of his family, once they met him and found out his name.

"Well, what is your top-secret last name?" I challenged him. "Mine is Starr, Allison Starr." I stuck out my hand for a corny shake. Cooper laughed and took my hand, pulling me closer.

"Perez. Cooper Ryan Perez," he said, then kissed me softly.

"Perez? Nope. Got nothing," I told him, then intensified the kiss. I wanted to tell him right then how I was feeling toward him, but I was a coward through and through.

I mean, come on, how often do summer loves last?

In the last week of my trip, Coop finally talked me into the water to experience surfing. The water was ice-cold even though the air around me was a balmy ninety-nine Southern California degrees. The thing that finally got me in the water was that I knew the proximity of where our bodies would be. Though we both had felt the undeniable connection, we were keeping strict physical rules. The chance to hold him as the water kept our bodies weightless gave me a thrill just thinking about it.

"Now don't get frustrated if you don't get up on the board," Coop was telling me as we bobbed up and down in the waves. I nodded and kept repeating what he had taught me; it became my mantra. Paddle, push, balance, stand. I was wearing a borrowed rash guard and lying on my stomach on the freshly waxed surfboard, keeping my eyes focused on the shoreline.

"You'll tell me when to go?" I could hear the fear in my voice. I'm academic, not athletic. Cooper laughed, and I felt his hand touch my leg as he moved in front of the board. He pushed himself closer and dipped me further into the cold water and lightly kissed the tip of my nose. When he spoke, he looked directly into my eyes.

"I told you I would. What else did I say?" I lost focus staring into those amazingly blue eyes.

"That it was going to be fun and fine," I repeated back to him like a good little parrot. He nodded and smiled.

"That's my girl," he said and floated off to my side. "Get ready," he said above the sound of the coming wave. "Now, Ali!" Cooper shouted. "Paddle!"

My arms pushed themselves deep into the water, and I moved them just as Cooper had shown me. After just a few seconds of paddling, it felt like I had been lifting weights in the gym for hours, but I kept going. I could feel the water raise the front of the board, and I readied myself to try to stand, focusing on my balance. I brought my legs up to tuck under my body, and I felt something tugging me back. As soon as my toes touched the board, the entire thing came shooting out from under me. Harsh cold water filled my nose and mouth. I couldn't tell which way was up, and I felt like I was going to drown. Pressure built in my lungs. I felt disoriented. I wanted to fight my way to the surface but couldn't find it.

Warm arms looped around my waist and eased me up. A moment later, my head broke the surface, and I coughed out seawater and gulped in air. Cooper was holding my back to his chest, and we were gliding toward the beach. My dark hair was covering my eyes, and I realized I was gripping his arms like they were my own personal life preserver.

"It's okay," Cooper's voice said into my ear. "I've got you."

I had hardly noticed that he was gliding the surfboard next to us until the ocean floor hit my feet. We'd made it. I put my feet down and tried to stand, but sometime during my near-death experience, someone must have replaced my legs with Jell-O because they could not hold my weight. Cooper's arms shifted under mine, and he nearly dragged me to the place where we had left our towels, leaving the board behind us on the sand.

"What happened?" I asked once I knew I was safe. The words were rough and painful in my throat. I pushed my hair off my face and looked to Cooper and found him staring at my foot. He was touching it lightly and pressing the surrounding area.

"Does this hurt?" he asked as he moved his hand around my ankle.

"No," I answered. "Should it?" He seemed satisfied with my answer and sat down next to me on his towel.

"It might later," he said, drying off. "It all happened so fast. You started paddling, and your foot got tangled in the leash. I don't think you realized that you were kicking your feet when you should have only been using your arms." This last part he said a little sympathetic, like he had done it before himself.

I felt tears burn in my eyes. "I told you I wouldn't be any good at this." I pouted as the feeling of humiliation set in. Cooper laughed easily and pulled me into his arms.

"You did just fine. It was an accident." He pressed his cold lips into my wet hair. "Next time will be much easier."

"No next time," I said defiantly. "If you want to off me, you better come up with a new way because I am not getting back into that liquid death trap." Cooper lay back onto the sand and rolled with laughter. I didn't know what he could possibly find so funny.

"Off you?" he managed to say in between gulps of breath. I crossed my arms over my chest and waited for him to gain his composure. Instead he pulled me down next to him and held me to his side.

"I have no idea why you think this is so funny," I demanded. "I almost died out there." In saying this, a whole new round of laughter started, and I was unable to resist laughing along with him. Despite how stupid I felt, my embarrassment melted away in the warm summer sun, laughing with Cooper. A moment later, we both lay on our backs, facing the bright sun. Cooper took my hand in his, and nothing needed to be said. We had found we could both enjoy the comfortable silence between us.

After a while, he said, "I told you I wouldn't let anything happen to you, didn't I?"

I rolled up to my elbow to get a better look at him. "Yes, you did," I admitted. I was alive, and the feeling that an elephant had stood on my chest had finally left. My back was aching, but it was nothing a hot bath couldn't fix. Cooper now mirrored my position except he shaded his eyes from the sun.

"Can I ask you something?" His voice was low and serious.

"Of course," I answered. He took pause, thinking before he spoke. Now *that* is a concept that I would love to master.

"Why would you say that?" he finally said. "About me wanting to off you, I mean?"

"Oh"—I shrugged with one shoulder—"in case you wanted to get rid of me without the messy breakup." Even as I said it, I could hear how ridiculous and childish it sounded, and I couldn't believe I had said it out loud. Cooper sat all the way up. He looked out into the water, his eyebrows pulled together in thought. *Think*, I told myself. There has to be some way to salvage this.

"I just thought that next week"—now was the time for honestly—"that this would be over for you," I said in a small voice. "That you would just move on to the real world, and I would go back to school." My stomach tied itself in knots as I spoke this truth. How was it possible that watching some cute local boy surf could turn into this? It had only been a few weeks, but I didn't know how I had managed without him.

"Over for me?" he answered and turned to face me. "Will it be over for you?"

I shook my head. "I don't think it will ever be over for me," I admitted. Cooper's features softened.

"I knew it," he whispered. "You were just trying to throw me off."

"Throw you off what?" I asked, which led me to wonder if it ever gets any less confusing trying to understand the male psyche.

"Allison Starr, don't you see?" He cupped my face in his hands. "I love you." Rocket ships soared inside me at his words. "You silly girl," he said, lips brushing mine as he continued, "I fell in love with you, and I can't tell my heart to stop just because summer is ending."

Cooper had made it sound so perfect and easy. "You love me?" I questioned. "Like, real love?" He laughed. Maybe it was the near-death experience or too much sun, but I needed to know if I heard him right.

"The kind that all great poets write about," he answered. Our noses bumped together, and I could feel my rational mind working in overdrive. It was now or never.

"Good, because I fell in love with you weeks ago." I rested my hands against his bare chest, pushing him back to see into his eyes. "Cooper Ryan Perez, I love you." Finally, I had said it out loud. Cooper searched my face, and before I could think another thought, he pulled me back to him, our mouths coming together feverishly. We moved in such synchronization that it was like it had been staged, but it was just another sign of how in tune we were.

Too soon he pulled away. We were both breathing unevenly, and our faces were flushed. I didn't want to say anything to undo this moment. His feelings were real—I hadn't imagined it. I felt Cooper's eyes on me, and

I turned to meet them. He raised his hand and brushed my wild, damp hair from my face.

"You are still beautiful, even though the ocean tried to take you down," he said, breaking the silence that hung between us. Neither one of us spoke about the future nor what it would bring us. Some things might be better left unsaid. We just sat there, holding each other close, not wanting time to pass as we watched the sun dip down into the now-orange water.

Time was passing whether we liked it or not, slipping though our fingers like the sand on the beach.

Four

Cooper

I told Allison that I loved her. Which I do, more than I wanted to admit, even to myself. I couldn't think about not seeing her every day. She has become a part of who I am now. We had the discussion about age a few weeks ago. We are three years apart, but she will be eighteen in a few months, so things won't seem so out of balance for us. Not that it feels unbalanced—I guess it will just be less frowned upon by society. I explained to her how it was that I was so much further along in school. Accelerated classes since my sophomore year paired with college classes since my junior. I'll still need to take some classes for my master's degree, but I can teach like I have always wanted to.

I was on my way to pick up Ali for our last night together. I had a surprise for her that took me a week to plan, and I was nervous because it all depended on Sean pulling through for me. I never thought crazy Trudy's house would become familiar to me, but it has. I knocked on the door, and Ali opened it quickly like she had been waiting for me. Her smile lights up my world.

"Hi," she says with a blush. Gosh, I love that blush.

"Hi," I say back and pull her close, and I don't want to let her go, but I can hear some noise deep in the house.

"Is that Ryan?" Trudy yells from somewhere. Ali leans back and smiles at me.

"Of course it is, Aunt Trudy." I can tell she is holding her patience. There is some bumping and clatter; then she appears. Trudy has paint on her face, and her graying hair is in a bun on her head.

"Ryan," she coos. I let Ali go and hug the crazy aunt. "Well, come in," she says. Allison shrugs, and I step inside.

"Aunt Trudy, we talked about this," Ali says with her eyes pleading. I smile, I do love this girl.

"Ali, be a doll and go find my glasses," Trudy says. "They're in my room." I can tell Ali wants to say something but decides against it and disappears. Trudy turns slowly toward me.

"I am assuming you have something you want to say to me, beautiful Trudy?" I ask quietly, attempting to butter her up. Her answer is a mischievous smile.

"I like you, Ryan, and I know how Ali feels about you," she starts. "I just want to say my piece, then be on your way." I nod. "She has been through a lot of pain, and I can't bare it if she is hurt again."

"Trudy, I would never—" She holds up her hand.

"I know, Ryan, I know. It is just it is your last night together, and I know that there might seem some pressure to . . ." She looked down, then back to me. "You know, seal the deal or something." *Oh my gosh. I could literally die right now.* Instead I just nod politely. "Just, be careful, okay?"

"Trudy." I clear my throat. "I love your niece and respect her, and just so you know, there are no plans to . . ." I can't even say the words.

"I can't find your glasses anywhere," Allison said as she came back into the room—thank God. She looked between the two of us, probably sensing the awkwardness. "You ready?" she asks, locking her beautiful brown eyes on to mine.

I reached for her hand. "Yes, I am." I glanced at Trudy, hoping she doesn't misinterpret that, but she just nodded as we left. Once in the truck, Ali turned toward me.

"Would you like to share with me what that was all about?"

I smiled, embarrassed. "Your aunt wanted to know if we were planning on, you know—how did she say it?—'seal the deal' tonight." Ali put her head in her hands and groaned.

"I am so embarrassed and so sorry," she said through her fingers. I pulled the truck to the curb once we were around the corner. She didn't look up, and I could see the red in her face. I touched her hand, and she flinched away. That was a first.

"Look at me please," I pleaded.

"I can't." Her voice is shaking. I pull her hands away from her face, and her eyes are tightly closed. I pull her across the seat and hold her close. I could smell the coconut scent that just seemed to be part of her. I kiss her neck and rub small circles on her back, trying to coax her into relaxing.

"You can talk to me," I encourage. Ali sits up and gains composure.

"Later," she said quickly. I watch her and decide she wasn't ready to talk now, but I would make her open up to me later. We drove in silence toward the beach and the surprise I've planned for tonight. I keep glancing at Ali from the corner of my eye. She keeps biting her finger and looking out the window; she looks upset. I want to know what is going on in that big brain of hers, but she closed up like a clam. I want her to be able to talk to me, to trust me with her feelings.

Tonight I am taking Allison to the place where this all began for me. She may not realize that day we first saw each other, but I saw her before she noticed me.

This small part of the beach changed my life, and the girl holding my hand changed my heart. My heart that completely belongs to her. Where my emotions turned from amazement to love. I need Ali to know what she means to me, what impact she has had on my life. To have her know that I'm never going to stop loving her no matter how much distance it put between us.

The sun was just starting its nightly descent into darkness. Her hand is in mine, and I can't help but notice how it just fits there. Ali keeps looking at the big orange sun, and I can tell she is deep in thought. Maybe now I can get her to open up to me.

"Hey," I finally say as I bump my shoulder into hers, breaking her silence. Not brilliant, but it was the first thing that popped into my head and made it out of my mouth.

"Hmm," was her response, which made me laugh. It was like she had forgotten I was there.

"Where did I lose you?" I stopped walking and turned her toward me, holding her shoulders in my hands.

"We are racing the sun," she mused. I arched an eyebrow, trying to follow her train of thought. "Like in the end of *Dracula*. They raced the sun too, but it was so they could kill the count."

"Okay," I said slowly. Ali blushed and looked down.

"One romantic walk on the beach—check. One incredibly perfect guy—double check. One moronic girl who doesn't know when to keep her mouth shut—overabundant amount of checks." I shook my head and kissed her nose.

"And that part of the book reminds you of us now?" I forced a smile, still trying to understand where she was coming from.

"No." She shook her head. "I feel silly for saying that—all of that. No, just how that was the only book I finished while I was here, and at the end, the sun closed that story . . ." Her voice trailed, and her gaze averted back to the sun.

"Hey, Ali," I say, shaking her slender shoulders in my hands. "When this sun sets, it's not our end. Okay?" I nodded, hoping she understood. "*Dracula* is fictional, and we are real people." I kiss her quickly.

"Part of me feels like this isn't real," she says sheepishly. "That tomorrow I will wake up and all of this would have been a dream."

"It would've been a good dream then." I pull her to my chest and hold her there, wanting this moment to never end.

She sighs and kisses my shoulder. "The best dream I've ever had," Ali says into my shirt. We just stand there, holding each other as we watch the sun simmer as it dipped into the Pacific Ocean. I want to tell her how much she means to me. How I never thought I could meet someone like her. Someone who can make me a better person and see the world in a whole new way.

"I have a surprise for you," I whisper into her ear. I take her hand and start to lead her to the tree line.

"What is it?" Curiosity and excitement are leaking in her question.

I keep leading her forward. "A surprise," I answer, stopping and turning her so she can't see what is set up. "This is where I first saw you," I tell her, "where it all changed for me." She nods, looking around, and I can see that she is holding on to her emotions as best she can. I can see Sean; he has pulled through for me, and he gives me a thumbs-up. "Close your eyes." Ali tilts her head to look at me suspiciously but does what I have asked of her. I wrap an arm around her slim waist and put my hand over her eyes.

"What is going on here?" She grabs my arm at her midsection and pulls me closer. It is almost dark now, and I can see the hard work Sean did pulling this off for me. I put my lips on Ali's neck.

"A surprise," I answer with a kiss. She turns her face, and I kiss her perfect lips. I can get lost in these kisses, and I almost do. I open my eyes and find that my stage is set. Sean is just waiting, and I motion him with my eyes to leave. After a minute of silent battle, he gets the hint. I wait until I know he is out of sight. I even watch as he gets in his car and pulls out of the dark parking area. We are now totally alone. I lead Ali to a blanket that has been set up.

"Ready?" I ask. She nods, placing her hands, which is still covering her eyes, on mine. I uncover her eyes and take a small step back. "Open them."

I am standing behind Ali, so I don't know what she is thinking. Spread out in front of us is a candlelit picnic. I'm not just talking about little tea light candles in those silver tins. I had Sean set up and light about fifty white pillar candles in the sand. In the center of it is a dark blanket with a picnic basket toward the edge. I want Ali to say something—anything. The silence is killing me. I reach out to touch her shoulder as she turns around.

"Cooper," she whispers, tears brimming at her dark lashes, "how did you do all of this?" Her voice is filled with wonder.

I moved closer and bent to whisper into her ear. "Magic." Ali giggles, and a tear slides down her cheek. I pull her into me, kissing her with all my emotion. I can feel her damp cheeks as the tears keep coming. I pull back to look into her eyes, finding them filled with tears, but I don't know if they're happy or sad.

"What is it?" I cup her face in my hands, and she closes her eyes. "Allison, please," I plead. Finally, she locks her gaze with mine.

"I love you," she says slowly. I nod and keep quiet, hoping she'll say more. "I don't want to be away from you, and tomorrow I will be." I know exactly how she is feeling, but I feel like I should be the strong and optimistic one for her.

"We still have tonight," I answer, quietly wishing that tonight would freeze us here. For a while, neither one of us speaks; no words can make this any easier. I watch the candles twinkle around us, like stars in the sky, and I am lucky enough to hold an angel in my arms. Ali mumbles something about being cold, so we sit on the blanket, and I cover her with the extra one I packed and pull her close.

"This is so beautiful," Ali says dreamily.

"I packed some food, if you're hungry," I mention. Ali leans back to look at me.

"You know me, always ready to eat." She smiles.

This girl rocks my world. I love that she isn't afraid of eating or speaking her mind. Most girls are so illusive that you never know exactly where they stand. Ali has always been straightforward and herself. Maybe I should tell her about my family. The money and trust funds waiting for me. Maybe that is why it is so easy to be with her—she doesn't know that side of me. I am almost certain she wouldn't care.

We pick at the food I had Sean set up for us tonight—cheese and crackers, fruits and a few vegetables, and chocolate-covered strawberries. I was thinking about a bottle of champagne but decided on good ol' apple cider since we both don't like drinking. They weren't large portions of food, but man, it filled me up. Or it could have been my nerves filling up my stomach. I lay back on the blanket and watched Ali sip the cider from her red plastic cup. I touched the small of her back, feeling the heat from her skin, and let my fingers explore the skin under the edge of her shirt. It is so soft and warm as my fingers traced her spine.

Ali turned to look at me, her eyes liquid. "That feels so good." Her eyes are closed, and she is almost purring at my touch.

"Do you want to talk to me about earlier?" I probe. I felt Ali's muscles tense under my hand.

"Nope," she answers quickly. I sat up and pulled her close. Leave it to Trudy to put doubts in our heads. I hadn't planned on taking it to that level with Ali—yet. I mean, yeah, I've thought about it—I am just a man.

"Were you thinking that maybe . . . maybe tonight . . . we'd . . . ?" My hands start to sweat, and I become riddled with nerves. Ali groans with embarrassment and falls backward onto the blanket, covering her face. I didn't know what to say, so I didn't say anything. It stuns me that she thought about being intimate with me and boosts my ego a little too.

"Yes," she finally said, though it was muffled under her hands. "I was hoping." I would be lying if I didn't admit my anticipation level vamped up a few notches. I leaned on my elbow next to her. With my free hand, I lifted hers from her face, but Ali kept her eyes closed. So I kissed her lids.

"I thought about it too," I admitted in hushed tones. Ali slowly opened her eyes. Neither of us moved. My face hovered above hers, locked in her gaze. Ali's hand touched my face lightly.

"I'm in love with you," she whispered. We lay there, side by side, bathed in moonlight, surrounded by candlelight. Ali moved slowly, pulling my face to hers. I let her kiss me, and it was the most sensual thing I have ever experienced. Her leg came over my body, placing her on top of me, and her hands were under my shirt.

I am only human.

I pull her flat to my chest and rolled, so we changed positions. Ali's arms tangled around my neck, and her mouth became almost desperate against mine. I kissed my way from her mouth to her collarbone, Ali's hands roaming all over my chest. She started tugging at the fabric and lifted my shirt off over my head. I looked down into her big brown eyes, and they were hungry.

Before I knew exactly what I was doing, I had my hands on Ali's stomach and was slowly taking her top off. She shifted, and her top was in my hand. Ali pulled my mouth back to hers, and we rolled once more, and her delicate body pressed into mine. One of her hands left my arm and moved to the fly of my pants; she was fumbling to unbutton them. I had to react while I was still able think.

"Ali." I wrapped my fingers around her wrist, stopping her.

"Cooper," she whispered, kissing my neck. Oh. My. God. Every hormone in my body went into overdrive. *Focus.* I took in a deep breath and rolled her over so we lay side by side again. We both lay, panting for air. After a minute, which I could have used a very cold shower, I sat up to look at her. Taking her hand in mine, I kissed it softly.

"You know that I want to do this, very much, but not tonight," I tell her.

Ali nodded, closing her eyes, which shut me out to her emotions. We both put out shirts back on and try to regulate my breathing and remind myself why I felt the need to stop this hot girl from taking advantage of me. Allison has the most perfect body, and I guarantee this will haunt my dreams for weeks.

"I just thought, with all the candles and it being our last night that you wanted me."

"Oh, I do, Ali, just not tonight." Oh man, I do, but I respect her too much and want to be able to wake up next to her and not have to say good night. Ali sits up and nuzzles into my side. I never want to let her go. I kiss the top of her head and keep her in my arms.

"Coop," Allison mummers, and I lean back and find her eyes serious. I touch her creamy, soft cheek, wondering what has caused so much concern.

"What is it?" I hope I don't sound too alarmed. I'm just so nervous that I've upset her.

"I'm just . . . worried . . . that maybe you should know." She fumbles with her words and turns away from me. Fear clenches at my chest.

"Ali"—I touch her back—"talk to me." She doesn't turn around, but I can hear her whisper something. I try to turn her toward me. "I can't hear you, sweetheart." Suddenly, she stands up, her fists in balls at her sides. She looks upset—not so much angry, just distressed.

"I'm a virgin," she reveals, her voice carrying in the dark. Before I can respond, she turns and runs, disappearing in the darkness.

"Ali." My voice is shaking. So this is what has been on her mind all night. With me saying no, she is probably feeling unwanted or that she did something wrong. I jump to my feet and take off in the direction she ran.

I can see her not far ahead; the moon is so bright tonight it almost seems like a spotlight. I call her name again, but she doesn't stop. I pick up my speed and am suddenly thankful for all the times Sean drags me to the gym with him. She knows I am close and that I can outrun her. Her run turns into a walk as she places her hands on her hips.

"I don't want to talk about it," she huffs out. I reach and take hold of her shoulder, spinning her around.

"Too bad, because I do." My voice is pleading, which shocks her. "You should know"—I close my eyes and know I need to be honest with her— "that I am too." Ali's eyes betray her thoughts, and I can see she doesn't believe me. Heck, Sean doesn't believe me either, but it is the truth.

"I hadn't found the right person yet." I move closer pushing some loose strands of hair off her face. I can see that Ali had been crying, and I move a step closer, putting my hands on her hips.

She looks confused as she looks into my eyes. "Then why did you stop?" I sigh, trying to figure out the best way to say this. I am guy raised with old world morals that some people just don't understand anymore.

"Because I think the first time should be special," I whisper, not trusting my voice at a normal range. "I don't think I could bear to be so close to you tonight and know I couldn't wake up next to you tomorrow morning." Even in the moonlight, I can see her cheeks blush. "When it is the right time, Ali, I don't want to have to say goodbye. I want to hold you until you fall asleep and see how your hair slips across your pillow." I lift my hand and touch her hair, letting it spill though my fingers. "I want to be there to see the sun light the bedroom and kiss you until you wake up." I bring Ali's hand to my lips and kiss it. "When the time is right"—I move so my lips are inches from hers—"it will be forever."

I lean in and kiss Ali as gently as I could manage, thinking of her as a fragile porcelain doll. At first she is hesitant but then melts into me, letting me wrap my arms around her. I fell more in love right then under that huge white moon. Ali's hands slid up my back and into my hair, holding my mouth to hers. She shivered, but I didn't know if she was cold or if the blood was pumping though her like it was with me. Without words, we walked back to our candlelit hideout.

When Ali sat back on the blanket, I wrapped the extra one around her shoulders. I couldn't take my eyes off her, and I found her looking at me the same way. She opened the blanket, and I opened it so we could both cuddle under it. Our bodies were so close it was hard to remember that we admitted our innocence to each other. Nothing I am thinking is innocent right now. I look into Ali's eyes, hoping she can't read my mind, but I can see it in her eyes.

"I love you so much," she whispers. What I hear is *"I want you so bad."* The endless difference between guys and girls. I kiss her forehead and hold her against me.

"I love you," I say into her hair. Ali sighs and presses her face into my neck.

"I really want to do it still." She tilts her head to look at me. I don't know what to say. I look into her eyes, and they say it all—they are smoldering hot and filled with desire.

"You don't have anything to prove to me," I assure her.

Ali searches my honest face like she is a human polygraph checking to see if I'm telling her the truth. She bites her lips, then slightly nods her head. "I think I need to leave you with part of me so we can't forget our summer."

My brain decides it needs a vacation, and my body takes over. Ali lurches and is on top of me like a cheetah attacking its prey—she is hungry. She kisses me like it is our last day on Earth, her hands exploring under my shirt, which she all but rips off. Ali kisses her way down and across my chest, her fingers tracing where her lips have been, and it is like fire burning me—a fire I don't want to put out.

My brain tries to come back from its break, but my body tells it to get out of town. Brain insists that I need to stick to my morals, but body reminds me that I won't see Ali for a long time. Brain says something stupid about absence making the heart grow fonder, but body has a comeback like "Shut up." All the while that this silent debate is going on, Ali hasn't stopped kissing my exposed chest. Then she says something that shocks me. First she sits up and, without warning, takes her tank top back off.

"Do you want to return the favor?" I felt like a cartoon character. I'm sure my eyes were bugging out of my head and puffs of smoke were shooting from my ears as body wins this round. I pushed Ali on her back on the blanket and immediately started to kiss her flat stomach. I braced myself by having a hand on either side of her as I kissed my way across her abdomen. The best part was the little sounds Allison was making, small moans and sighs. I started to kiss my way up so that eventually I would make contact with her mouth and instantly realized as I reached her breasts that Ali's body had gone rigid.

"Cooper . . . wait." Her words came out strained. I sat up to look at her. In her internal debate of brain versus body, brain won. "You were right," she says and sits up, pushing me back. "Tonight isn't the night."

Did you hear that, body? Time to cool down fast—like it or not. "I'm sorry," she adds, and you can hear the guilt her apology is coated in.

It takes me a moment before I can talk. "Don't be sorry." My voice is husky and rumbles in my throat. For the second time that night, we both pull our discarded clothes back on—except this time, Ali won't look at me. "Hey." I touch her arm.

"I'm so sorry," she says again. I shake my head and pull her into me before she can bolt.

"There is no reason to say sorry." I kiss her hair and just hold her close.

"Yes, there is. I've been acting crazy tonight. Running away, then trying to jump you." She shakes her head. "I just feel like everything is changing and slipping away. It was the only way I could think to hold on to this." Her fingers dig into my sides .

"Things are changing, and we can't do anything about that. But if you are worried about us"—I lean to look at her—"what we have won't change. We have a very long time stretched in front of us." Ali smiles and puts her head on my shoulder.

The candles are starting to burn out, but neither of us makes a move to leave. We just hold each other, holding on to all the time we have left together. Ali yawns and tries to hide it. "Are you tired?" I ask the obvious question.

"No," she answers, her voice defiant as another yawn escapes. I understand.

"We'll be together again soon," I promise.

"Not soon enough." I couldn't agree more.

The moon is high in the dark sky, telling us that it is time to leave the spot where I first found and fell in love with Allison. It was the last thing I wanted to do, but it's almost midnight, and we have an early morning tomorrow. She helps me pack up the picnic and carry it back to my truck. We don't say much on the drive back to Trudy's. We don't need words to express the feelings out loud because they were almost tangible in the space around us.

I walk Ali to her door and kiss her softly under the porch light.

"I love you," she whispers into my lips.

"I love you, Ali," I responded. "I'll see you in the morning." I would rather just carry her up to her bed, tuck her in, and hold her all night. But I left the girl I had fallen in love with this summer at her front door and went home.

When I got home, my mom was still up, waiting for me.

"Did you have a nice night with Allison?" she asked quietly. I hug and kiss my mom.

"Yeah," I tell her, not wanting to relive everything that happened tonight. "What are you still doing up?" Mom is usually in bed by nine, and it is after midnight, so something must be going on. I take a seat next to her.

"Waiting for you to get home." She smiles, but it is filled with stress.

"What is it, Mom?" I don't like when she is so cryptic like this. She takes a sip of her wine, stands up, kisses the top of my head, and hands me a piece of paper. I take the note but wait to open it until I am alone.

It's a handwritten note, a message Mom took earlier tonight.

> *Chico Prep Charter Junior High School called and wants to offer*
> *you a job in their English department. They need to hear from*
> *you ASAP. It sounds like a really good opportunity even though*
> *it is further than what you would have liked. Think about it.*
> *Love you son.*

I folded the paper and put it on the kitchen counter. I had just been handed my dream job that would take me over five hundred miles away from my dream girl.

I didn't notice that Mom had come back in the kitchen. I didn't notice that I had been staring at the same spot on the wall for a half an hour either. Mom must sense the struggle in my heart as she sits back down next to me.

"They said you could e-mail your response with any questions," she tells me. I nod and force a smile. "It is the opportunity you have worked so hard to get, Cooper. I know you'll make the right choice." She stands and hugs me, trying to give me support. "See you in the morning." I know my mom will support whatever choice I make; she has always wanted me to choose my own path, but I still feel the responsibility to make her proud.

Once in my room, I sit in front of my laptop for almost an hour before I can respond to the offer. I type my reply:

I, Cooper Ryan Perez, would like to accept the position you have offered at Chico Prep Charter Junior High School.

Five

Allison

I couldn't sleep at all tonight. I tried to, but I could never get comfortable. Oh, and I was pretty hot and bothered replaying my beach make out scene over and over. Cooper and I had the sex talk tonight. It wouldn't have been a bad thing if I hadn't thrown myself at him, admitted my innocence, and then ran away from him in pure embarrassment. So much for being mature. He was so incredible about everything that it made me want him even more, but he was right. It'll be worth the wait.

It has to be around four in the morning. I decide sleeping is just not in the cards tonight, so I tiptoe my way into the kitchen to make myself some hot tea. To my surprise, Aunt Trudy is sitting at the table, reading her newspaper.

She watches me as I entered the cluttered little space. "I couldn't sleep either," she tells me. I sighed not, wanting to speak. I feared that once I realized that this was it, I would break down into an ocean of tears. I poured hot water over a tea bag and watched as the liquid caused the contents of the sachet to seep. Slowly the water changed color, and the fragrance filled the air.

"You really do love him, don't you?" Aunt Trudy asked quietly. I nodded but didn't turn around for fear that spoken confirmation would surely lead to tears. "Then love will find a way, honey, trust me." I finally turned to look at her. The emotion in her eyes made it real for me. I trusted her words.

I took my tea back to my room to write Cooper a letter. Yesterday my aunt had given me a packet of pictures she had taken over the summer—most of them of me and Cooper, or me and her. I picked through them until I found the one she insisted on taking right as we left on our first date. We both looked excited and filled with raw emotion. Then I found one taken just a day or so ago, and our expressions were the same. Nothing had worn off over the weeks we had spent together. I set the pictures so I could glance at them as I wrote.

Dear Cooper,

I cannot possibly put into words what this summer has meant to me, what it'll always mean to me. I never thought anything like this would happen...especially to me. My world is forever changed for the good because you are in it. I will miss not seeing you every day no matter how brave a face I put on. I know we will work something out and see each other soon. I look forward to exchanging emails and learning more and more about you. It might be easier for me to open up with the barrier of a computer screen between us and learn to trust my feelings and heart to someone.

I will learn to be patient. I will learn to trust. I will learn the meaning of love to its very roots.

Cooper, I know we haven't known each other very long, but I know myself and how I feel for you. I feel full and weightless all at the same time. I know I love you and I trust my heart to you. Carry it with you wherever you go, it is yours.

All the love in the world,

Ali

I read and reread my letter. I folded it around a picture of us on the beach, the ocean stretching out behind us. I packed the rest of my things, then carried it all downstairs. I could hear Aunt Trudy speaking softly to someone. I glanced at the clock on the wall, which is ticking loudly; it read half past five. I try to match my breathing with the steady ticktock, it being steadier than the thumping in my chest. I took my mug back to the kitchen and was surprised at what I found—Cooper sitting with my aunt! They both turned slowly toward me, their conversation ceasing. Cooper smiled, but it didn't touch his eyes; it was more of a sad smile.

"I found him outside," Aunt Trudy finally said when she realized neither of us could speak. "He was just sitting out all alone in the dark, looking all miserable, so I had to let him in."

"Hi," Cooper says to me. I swallowed a lump in my throat that I didn't know was there.

"Hi," I repeated and cleared my throat. Aunt Trudy was slowly moving toward the kitchen doorway.

"Well, I better go get ready," she said. "We'll leave in about an hour."

With that, we were alone. Neither of us spoke or moved for a full minute. I blushed, thinking about how I had acted last night. Seduce, run, then seduce again—not my best moment. I still had the letter I wrote him in my hand, so without thinking, I just held it out in front of me. Cooper stood and crossed the room. Ignoring my outstretched arm, he took my face in his hands and kissed me.

It started gentle and soft, then quickly built. Before I knew how I had gotten there, my back was pressed to the pantry doors. Cooper was everywhere. His hands, his mouth, his breath, and I wanted more. I grabbed at him and pulled him closer, never wanting to let go. I deepened the kiss as I slipped my hands under the back of his shirt. Cooper pulled his head back, and his eyes were dark blue, like sapphires, and he looked how I felt—hungry.

His voice was hoarse as he spoke into my ear. "I want you." His mouth moved down my neck, then across my jaw. Coop's hands have been on my hips, holding me close to him, but now they are touching my shoulders and sliding lightly over my collarbone.

"What about what you said last night?" I managed to say in broken breaths. Cooper brought his mouth back to mine, and I wrapped my arms around his neck. *Got it. Forget about the waiting thing—I like this plan.*

"Allison, don't forget to call your dad before we leave!" Aunt Trudy yells from upstairs, though it sounds like it's from the next room.

Cooper takes a step back and closed his eyes and ran his hands through his hair. *Wait. No. Don't stop yet.*

"I'm sorry, Allison," he finally says. Which I hate when someone apologizes and you don't know why. Especially after some serious kissing.

"I'm not complaining," I answered boldly. "I'm the one who tried to, you know, on the beach last night." This made Cooper laugh, which is a good sign considering the tense emotions in the room. He had walked to the opposite side of the small kitchen, and his back was to me. Uh-oh. This cannot be good.

"That isn't what I am sorry about." He crossed the room, taking my hands in his. He picked up the letter that had fallen to the floor and slid it into his back pocket. I tilted my head, and he continued, "I had a message when I got home last night about a job."

"That's good." I tried to sound hopeful, though his face gave me no hope.

"I am going to be teaching at a private school in Chico, a couple hours above Sacramento." He took a breath. "It's farther than what I would have liked, but I had to take it." I touched his cheek and kissed his mouth.

"Is that all?" I asked, trying to mask the minor hysteria in my voice. "Because it sounded much more serious." Cooper smiled, and I cupped his cheek in my hand. "Like you said, it'll all work out somehow. Trust in this." Then I placed my hand over his heart.

"I love you, Allison," he told me as he took me in his arms. Ten seconds, or maybe an hour, later, Aunt Trudy came back downstairs, letting us know that it was time to go.

Cooper rode to the train station with me and Aunt Trudy. We exchanged the letters we had written—mine was just one simple envelope; his was a huge envelope packed with many letters. I hate goodbyes. I try to avoid them since I lost my mom. She died almost ten years ago at the age of forty. It was sudden, an unknown heart condition. I said goodbye to her about fifteen minutes before they pronounced her dead. She died in surgery; the damage to her heart was too great to repair. I had just turned eight. Since then, I avoid goodbyes. Deep down I've been afraid that saying goodbye is like giving someone a death sentence. Aunt Trudy knows how I feel about this, so I am not surprised when she mentions quietly to Cooper not to say it to me.

"Say something like 'See you soon,'" she whispers to him as I am managed my luggage, pretending not to hear. It is time for me to get on the train, and it is the last thing I want to do.

Aunt Trudy pulls me into her arms before I can think another thought. "Sooner and longer next time, kiddo," she says into my ear. I hug her tight.

"Next summer is all yours, Aunt Trudy. I love you." I hug her tighter, then release her. She steps back, and Cooper steps forward. We just stand there, not speaking. Neither of us wants to face this. Then it happens with no warning—my tears. Cooper pulls me to his chest.

"Hey, honey," he whispers, trying to soothe me. "We'll be together soon, and I'll call you tonight—I promise." I don't want to let him go.

"I love you," I mumble into his shirt. "I'll see you soon," I add. He laughs at this, and I wish I could capture that laugh in a jar to open and hear when I am alone.

"See you soon," Cooper says into my cheek and kisses me. All too soon, I am all alone on the train, holding the envelope with Cooper's letters inside with both hands. I'm just waiting for the train to pull away before I rip it open. I slowly open the envelope. Inside were five letters and a small box. I held all the letters in my left hand and the box in my right. I shook the box, and it clattered with the contents. It was labeled "Open the night before the first day of school." The others were dated, and one had today's date on it. I tore it open.

> *Dearest Allison,*
>
> *My heart is breaking without you not at arm's reach. I didn't know I could feel like this so quickly. What we have is real and set in stone. No distance will keep us apart. We will be together soon, but not soon enough. Please never let doubt seed your thoughts about us.*
>
> *For stony limits cannot hold love out, and what love can do that dares love attempt.*
>
> *(Romeo and Juliet Act 2, Scene 2)*
>
> *We can get through anything that life throws at us. You have forever changed me and gave life to my heart. I will never forget our time falling in love at the beach, under the sun of summer.*
>
> *Until I can hold you again,*
>
> *Cooper Ryan Perez*

I held the neatly printed note to my chest and realized tears streaked my cheeks. It's clear that we were both on the same page with our feelings. I just selfishly wish he wouldn't be so far away for work. I know I put up a strong front being brave and all, but come on. He said he was over five hundred miles away. The next time I'll be able to see him is Thanksgiving. I'll be eighteen by then, which is good, but it still seems so far away. I lean my head back and close my eyes, remembering every detail of Cooper's face.

"Ma'am." Someone was shaking me. I opened my eyes to find myself at my stop. I gathered my things and got off the train. I could see my dad waving to me; he is hard to miss. My dad, Robert, is six foot five and all muscle. He is the captain of the county fire department and spends more time away from home than we both would like. Even with the long hours, my dad has always been there for me, and he works hard to hide the pain that haunts him. The ache of carrying the love for someone he'll never see again. Dad makes his way to me quickly and has me off my feet in a hug in no time.

"My Ali-Oops," he said, calling me by my nickname. "I've missed you so much."

I hugged him tight. "I missed you too, Dad." He carried my bags, and we headed home.

Cooper called me that first night as promised, and we e-mailed each other twice a day. I told him more about my parents, and he told me about his family. It was difficult telling him about my mom, how I lost her so early and my fear of forgetting her. Cooper listened and opened himself up to me by confiding that his family is wealthy, which in turn he has kept people at a distance—until me. He was now in Northern California, and school would start in two days for both of us. Cooper told me he'd call me after school; he had lots to do with lesson plans. This will be the longest we've had to go not speaking since we met. He told me to open the small box that had been packed with all my letters. I wasted no time getting it open.

Inside was a charm bracelet made of petite keys strung together on a leather cord. Every key was different, like each one unlocked something separate. I put it on immediately. It sounded like I had a miniature wind chime on my wrist, and the sound was lovely. I e-mailed Cooper, knowing he wouldn't be able to respond, telling him how much I loved it. I asked him if there was a story behind it; it looks like it has been passed down. Maybe a family heirloom, which equals a new sort of seriousness in our relationship. Which in turn means I need to text my best friend and get her input on what all this could mean.

Key to his heart? –C

But there are so many. –A

There was no note? –C

No. I emailed him for answers. -A

I didn't get a response back from my e-mail to him until the morning of my first day of school. I really wish I would have spent less time on my hair this morning so I could have read it. Instead I printed the response and tucked it in my backpack as I left for school. I had called Christina, my best friend, from San Diego and told her all about Cooper. At first she was wary, but then she became supportive the more I told her about my surfer boy. Christina and I have been best friends since elementary school; she is like a sister to me. She was waiting outside so we could go to school together on our first day as seniors. Her music was up so loud that I could hear it through the windows. Christina was dancing in her car and laughing.

"Seniors!" she yelled as I opened the door. I started to laugh and climbed in. As I did, she immediately grabbed my wrist to examine the bracelet.

"This is super retro cute." Christina's dark green eyes were sparkling. "It totally has to mean something." I buckled my seat belt, and she hit the gas as we headed toward Chino Prep Charter High School for our senior year.

We were both jittery with excitement as we walked onto campus, and we weren't the only ones. Our entire class was keyed up for our last year of mandatory learning. I was just anxious to make it through the day and get home because I knew Cooper would be calling me.

During every class, I tried to read Cooper's e-mail but quickly became bombarded with assignments. By lunch I heard the buzz that our old and cryptic English teacher, Mr. Snyder, had retired and that the new teacher was a fox. I couldn't care less except that I was the senior class English tutor and would work hand in hand with this new teacher. English was my last class of the day, seventh period, so I guess that is when I would see what all the fuss was about. I went to sixth period with determination to read the e-mail that I had been trying to read since seven a.m.

Luckily I have Mrs. Sinclair sixth period, chemistry, and she wanted us to talk to our lab partners about our summer. Christina is my partner; this is the only class we have together, and she told me to read the e-mail and then fill her in. Finally, I pulled out Cooper's printed words. It wasn't very long. I read it once, then again.

Time stopped.

Christina looked at me. "Are you okay?" She touched my arm, then my face. Cold sweat covered my body, and my stomach twisted, and I thought I was going to be sick. I jumped up without thinking and ran for the girl's bathroom. I could hear Christina yell after me, but I couldn't stop. I locked myself in a stall and leaned against the door, Cooper's letter hanging in my hand. My heart thumped in my chest, and I was shaking.

I wasn't alone long. "Ali!" Christina called. She tapped on the stall door. "Let me in." With trembling fingers, I unlocked the door. She had both of our backpacks and wore a look of concern. "Is this about the e-mail?" Her golden brows knitted together in worry.

"Cooper," I managed to say as I handed her the paper. I should keep this to myself but knew if there was anyone to confess to, it was Christina. I could trust her with this, and I'd need a friend who would understand and be supportive. Christina took it, eyebrows now arching in surprise, and then scanned the sentences multiple times. She looked back to me, then pulled me into a hug.

"It will be okay," she said, her own voice trembling. I know she's just being nice. It will not be okay.

The e-mail said this:

Ali- There was a mix up. I am going to teach at Chino Prep Charter, not Chico. I will be a teacher at your school. We need to talk...I don't know how or if...I just don't know what to do. Cooper.

Six

Cooper

Every class that leaves moves me closer to the inevitable. I went to Chico Prep only to find out that there was a huge mix-up. I was supposed to say go to Chino Prep. As in Chino, where Ali lives. As in the school Ali attends. Not just teach there—when I received my attendance sheets, I found she was in my last class of the day and is also the senior English tutor. Which translates that not only will I be her teacher and have her in class for an hour, but I will also be required to see her three times a week while she tutors in my classroom.

My first question was, how the heck could this have happened? The answer was in Chico. There was a spot open in the history department, and the English opening was in Chino. The phone notifications were crossed, and the calls went to the wrong candidates. Brian Smith went to Chino to find himself in the same situation. Once they told me where I was actually supposed to be, I prayed I had heard wrong. No way I can teach at Allison's school, but I accepted, and I have to live with my choice until I can find something new. I only had time to send her a quick e-mail, then jump on a plane. Now I face the slow torture of her entering my classroom. Sheesh, my classroom. The hardest part of this is my absolute desire to see her combined with absolute terror. I hope that I can keep my wits about me and get through the final class of the day—Ali's class.

The bell rings, and the last class starts to trickle in. I don't even want to see her face when she walks in because I don't know if she got the e-mail I sent. I had the picture of us from this summer that she gave me in a letter—our last night together—on my desk. But it is now tucked safely in my top drawer. I sit on the edge of my desk and look over the plans I have for the first week. I decided to have the students read *Dracula* since it was what Ali was reading and one of my favorites—it would be a good starting point.

There are murmurs throughout the class. I was told by the basketball coach at lunch that all the kids in his class were talking about the young new guy—like I needed something else to make me nervous. A burst of giggles breaks out, and that's when I look up.

Ali is standing in the doorway, not looking up and unwilling to move. There are two open seats in the classroom, front row and back. The bell rings, and the students are supposed to be seated. Ali is still standing outside, looking like she might throw up. I am so conflicted. I want nothing more than to pull her close and tell her how much I love her. But I can't. I am not even supposed to know who she is. I am just staring at her, having no idea what to say.

A guy from the back of the class stands and goes to her. He puts his arm around her shoulder and whispers into her ear. I want to take his head off. Ali nods, still staring at the ground. The guy who is going to fail my English class keeps talking, and Ali smiles weakly. Finally, he is able to talk her into coming into class, and I am relieved. I realize that there are twenty pairs of eyes staring at me now, and I look up and smile.

"Welcome to senior English," I manage to say. "I'm Mr. Perez." Then I take roll. Jeremy Fisher is the guy who is sitting next to Ali. I pass around a seating chart, and everyone fills in their names. I look at it and just stare at Ali's handwriting for a moment. She handwrote the notes she gave me about a week ago, but now her letters seemed hard and strained, like her hand had been trembling as she wrote it.

"Okay." I set the paper down. "We are going to start this year off with *Dracula*." Then I jump into the lesson I have planned. All I can do is focus on the words of Bram Stoker. I outline what I expect from them and blah-blah-blah until the bell rings. All the students get up, except for two— Ali and Jeremy.

I watch him lean close and take her hand, leaning in and saying something to her. Ali responds in a whisper. Jeremy stands and leaves. Ali and I are alone. I walk to the closed door and prop it open, just slightly. She doesn't move at all, even as I move and sit in the desk next to her.

"I didn't know," I finally say. She nods. This is killing me. I move and kneel next to her. I can see that she is wearing the key bracelet I gave her. It was my grandmother's. She was always misplacing things, so my grandfather made it for her. The last key he put on was the key to a new house he had built for her. The key, he said, that would start their future. That's why I gave it to her. I see Ali as my future. She sent me an e-mail asking about it, but I was notified of the school mix-up, and I didn't respond. I want so bad to reassure her how much she means to me, but now I am bound by rules.

"We are supposed to be planning our approach for tutoring this year," she says, and I can see she is holding back tears as she takes out a spiral notebook. She clears her throat and takes in a long breath, and she still hasn't looked at me. "The beginning of the year is when we'll get the most interest, and . . ." Her hands are shaking. I put my hand over hers, and she seems to relax.

"Please look at me, Ali," I whisper. "I'm still me." I just want to see her big brown eyes and tell her everything will be okay.

"You are Mr. Perez," she says as her voice catches in her throat. "I am Allison Starr, your student." Tears rolled down her pink cheeks, and my heart starts to break.

"Ali," I said, moving closer. "I know this complicates things, but . . ." What could I say? As long as I am here as Ali's teacher, we can't be together. Finally, she looks at me. Her eyes are dull, but sparkling with tears. Her incredible lips are pouted out, and the bottom one is trembling. I can't stop myself from touching it. Ali's lips part open, and the tears keep coming. I cup her face with my hand, and her eyes close, and she leans into it.

"I need to go," she mutters but doesn't move. She locks her gaze with mine once again, and I'm drawn in. I lean in and press my lips to hers. After a quick moment, she leans back, stuffing all her things into her backpack, and runs from the room. I sit on the floor, alone and confused.

***

I am living in a hotel for now. I slump into the badly upholstered chair and power up my laptop. I stayed in my classroom for almost three hours, unwilling to leave in case Ali came back, but she never did. I brought up my e-mail. I have one from Ali. My heart beats an extra time or two as I open it.

Dear Cooper,

I opened your letter and it said to email you about how my first day of my last year of high school went. It was horrible. I found out that the guy that I love is unattainable. It doesn't help that every girl in my entire school is in love with the new English teacher and won't stop talking about him. He reminds me of this guy I met at the beach this summer. I am in love with that guy. The most horrible thing is it feels like my heart is literally breaking in my chest and I find it hard to breathe. Even more atrocious than that pain is the pain of being in love and knowing that it is over. I know it has to be over but desperately want to hold onto denial and find some way to make it work. I don't want to let him go, but he just got his dream job and I know what he will choose. I will chalk myself up to a summer crush and find some way to push on.

I hope your first day was better. I don't expect a reply. I have no expectations.

ASTARR

Ouch. I look at the time stamp, and she had just sent it a half hour ago. I need to talk to her, to explain to her that I had no idea. My hands are tied. Not just losing my job, but jail time, she is my underage student.

But I love her; that hasn't changed, and she needs to hear it. I send the e-mail I had written as a response to the key charm bracelet. The one I had planned on sending while I was five hundred miles away. I make the split decision to go to her. I am still that guy from the beach, and she deserves better than an e-mail trying to explain. I am on the road in no time and type her address into my GPS in my rental car. She only lives ten miles from where I am staying. Convenient.

I pull up in front of her house, and it is dark; there are no lights on except for one room upstairs. I sit and just stare, waiting for something to happen. I guess I am that something that needs to happen. I know that Mr. Starr works long hours and isn't usually home until after ten or eleven most nights, and it's only six. I am somehow at the front door, knocking before I know what I am doing. I knock and then knock again with sudden urgency.

"Coming!" I hear Ali yell from behind the door. She swings it open and then freezes. "You can't be here," she says, quickly closing the door halfway. Her eyes are red and puffy, and she is clenching a tissue in her fist.

"I am that guy from the beach," I almost yell. Her sad doe eyes widen. "My love for you hasn't changed, but we do need to talk about this. I'm not letting you just run away from this." I lower my voice.

Ali nods slowly and looks down the street, then opens the door so I can come in. I can feel the tension in the air, and all I can think about was our last night on the beach together filled with a completely different tension. We just stand there, three feet apart, not even looking at each other. Ali turns her back to me and takes a step away from the door where I am still standing.

"So I'm guessing that you came here to say something along the lines of 'I will always love you, but it's over' or something like that?" Her voice is low and defeated. I take a step closer and touch her arm.

"No," I say slowly, and Ali turns to look at me. "I came here to tell you that I love you." Her breath is caught in her throat. I am overwhelmed with emotion at the raw look in her eyes. "I love you, Allison Starr, always," I say, taking her in my arms, filling my lungs with air. It's like I haven't been able to breathe without her close. "I love you," I say one last time before I kiss her. I can tell that she is holding back. "It is me Ali, Cooper," I say, kissing her ear, letting my teeth graze her lobe. I feel her shiver against me.

"Cooper," she whispers in recognition and hearing her say my name is the sweetest sound on Earth. I nod, and her arms come around me, pulling me close. I know I should be here to tell her it's over, but it isn't. I don't think it will ever be over for either of us. So instead we make out like it's our last day of the planet. All the want and need from being apart has taken its toll, and we can't control ourselves. The next time we come up for air, it is about an hour later, and we are somehow in her bedroom. I roll over on my side, and so does she.

"How did we get in here?" I ask. Ali laughs, and I recognize it as the laugh before I became her *Mr. Perez.*

"I can't be positive, but I am pretty sure you carried me some of the way," she says, running her hands through my shortened hair. For the next hour, we are just Coop and Ali who fell in love over the summer. We kiss and laugh, and no problems loom over us. Our stomachs remind us of the simple things like the necessity to eat. We decide to go to the kitchen, and she makes me macaroni and cheese. I am surprised to see that it is almost nine.

"When is your dad coming home?" I finally have to ask. She looks at the clock.

"He is on a twenty-four-hour shift, so maybe around eight a.m."

Allison's dad is a fireman and has some crazy hours. He is the captain, so his hours are a little more structured, but he is always willing to go beyond the call of duty if it is for the greater good. At first all I can think about is that it gives us hours upon hours alone together, but the reality of my visit dawns on us.

"Ali," I start. She shakes her head.

"I'm not ready for this to be over yet." She stands and crosses the room, crossing her arms over her chest. I stand and follow her, holding her from behind.

"It isn't over," I assure her. "Just wait until we can figure out what to do." She turns and faces me.

"You are my teacher. They will fire you." She says it so direct and cold. "Or put you in jail."

I nod, not wanting to accept this. "I know."

"So," Ali finally says, "we are done." I can feel tears burning at my eyes.

"In the sense that I am not going to see anyone else until my girlfriend graduates in May." I kiss her hair. Ali lets out a hard laugh and a smile that doesn't touch her eyes. We kiss once more. It is very soft and sweet.

"I don't expect you to do that," she says as we walk to the door. I turn to make direct eye contact with her.

"I don't think you understand how much I truly love you." That blush that I love touches her cheeks. "You are the woman I love, and I am not going to date other people until that special day in May." I feel sick to my stomach saying this, knowing how much it will hurt to be away from her. "I do understand that this is your senior year, and you'll have events and dances, so . . ." I don't even want to finish my thoughts. Ali nods solemnly but doesn't answer.

"Okay." She smiles, but it still doesn't touch her sad eyes. I lift her chin, and I can see it—the separation. Ali is closing down and shutting me out. But what else can we do?

Seven

Allison

I never wanted to be the strong one, but I could see it in his beautiful blue eyes that September night, I had to be the one. Saying goodbye—no matter how temporary it may be—was one of the hardest things I had to do. I thought as the weeks went on that the pain would subside, but it only grew. Every day became a challenge if I could make it through or not. I have lost my appetite for life too. Nothing seemed to matter. I couldn't even seem to lose myself in the safety of my books.

Tutoring during the week was agony, being so close to Cooper but having to keep distance. All evidence of summer erased from his appearance. Gone was the carefree floppy-haired boy surfing away his days. Now a man with the weight of Atlas on his shoulders stands at the front of my class every day. His hair darker, the tan of his skin lightening. He looks like Cooper, but it just isn't the same person. My chest ached from being away from him, and I don't know how much longer I can justify my depression.

Being in a private school means there are less students, so everyone knows everyone's business, including things about teachers. We're teenagers, and we gossip—it's just what we do. About a week ago is when I first heard it. Mr. Perez and Ms. Sherman are dating. Two days later, it was rumored that they were engaged. Talk about a blow to the heart. Ms. Sherman, Stacy Sherman. She isn't just any teacher—she is the PE goddess of our school. I'm not exaggerating—Zeus could be her father. She is tall and slim with a tight muscular . . . everything. Her long blonde hair is always perfect to match the perfect tan she has year-round. She is a few years older than Cooper, but he doesn't seem to mind. I know this because I am a stalker. I waited by the faculty parking lot and watched them leave for lunch together. They were laughing, and he opened the door to his car for her, and she touched his arm and winked at him. Winked! She is a tramp. Ms. Tramp, and I have her fourth period just before lunch.

So much for "I'm not going to see anyone until May." Blah-blah—crap crap.

It has been almost three months, or sixty-eight days, since the last time we've been together. I should have savored every second of that last day we had, but I didn't grasp that it was our last day—our kiss. If I had, I may not have ever let him leave. It's the first week of December, and we've had almost no contact. Three weeks until winter break and I can mope all I want.

Coop—Mr. Perez has been extremely careful. He hardly calls on me in class, never makes eye contact for more than a second, and during tutoring, he keeps the door open and sits on the opposite side of the classroom. I, on the other hand, have been borderline depressed and obsessive. I replay every second we spent together. Now I have the joy of analyzing Ms. Sherman and comparing myself to her, and I never come out on top when I do. I don't think I slept or ate for the first month of school. He looks fine, more than fine. His hair is darker and a little longer, and he even has the nerve to have a bounce in his step. I sigh and realize Christina is watching me. We are in chemistry, and I have an hour with Mr. Hotness, as some of the girls have taken to calling him, in about twenty minutes.

"It has been months, Ali," she whispers almost urgently. I nod. "I mean he dumped you hard and acts like you don't even exist." She touches my hand lightly. "I hate to be the one to say it, but you need to move on." I pull my hand back from hers like she burned me.

"I don't want to move on," I mumble angrily.

"I know," she says and takes my hand, ignoring me. We listen to the rest of the lecture and then have lab time. Christina decides I need to spruce up a little and puts some blush on my sunken cheeks and gloss on my lips before English. When the bell rings, I am surprised to find Jeremy waiting outside of the door. Christina smiles and shrugs as she walks away. *That sneaky little . . . move on . . . Jeremy. Some friend she is.*

"Hey, Ali," Jeremy says, taking my backpack from my shoulder to carry it like he used to back when he was my boyfriend. "I thought we'd walk to class together."

"Okay," I say, feeling naked without my bag to hide behind.

Jeremy is a nice guy. We dated until the end of last year; we just thought it was better to break it off and enjoy our summers. It was mutual, but now I am thinking it was more my idea than his. Being back at school has made him sentimental or something. Jeremy had persistently kept in touch this summer, telling me he missed me, but I have been a ghost the last few months. Still, he has been telling me that he misses "us" and has been trying to take me out.

"So," he says as we get into an almost-empty hallway, "winter formal is in three weeks, and I heard you didn't have a date." I stop walking and look at him.

He is a good guy, cute too. But can't he see that I am broken? I have known Jeremy since elementary school, and he has always been my friend. I was there when he made varsity football our freshman year and went to every one of his games. He was the popular jock, and I was the nerd. He was sought after by all the girls in the school, and I couldn't lie to myself—I could see the appeal. Jeremy is average height, but loaded with muscles. His hair is the color of fresh brewed coffee, and his eyes are this intense amber brown that you can't help but get lost in.

Last year we just looked at each other and decided to give dating a try. It was strange at first, especially the first time he kissed me, but I also felt safe and wanted. It was strange walking hand in hand with him as he carried my backpack class to class, with everyone watching. I secretly wondered if we'd get married someday and tell our kids how we met in the sandbox, friends all our lives. In the end, I realized he'd always be my friend, and he had gained a new perspective in what he saw in me. He told me the night we broke up that I am the love of his life.

"I'm not going," I tell him flatly. He takes my hand in his and keeps walking. I want to snatch my hand back, but it feels so warm, and I feel that wanted feeling. Immediately, people turn to watch us. I'm sure we will be rumored to be back together by first period tomorrow. Right before we enter our English class together, he turns me toward him.

"Please just think about it," he says, amber eyes pleading. "I'm asking you to please go to our senior winter formal, Ali. Even if it is only as friends." Jeremy leans in and lightly brushes his lips to my cheek, then walks into class. I can feel eyes on me, two of them blue and burning fiercely, as I take my seat. The entire class saw and heard everything between Jeremy and me, and I know my face has to be the color of a tomato. Great.

Jeremy puts my bag on my desk, and I slowly look up. Cooper looks upset and gives me a look that chills my heart. He told me to go to school events. He is the one who won't even speak to me. How can he be angry at me? The bell rings, and I sit in my hard plastic chair.

"Don't unpack your things," Mr. Perez says. "We will be spending this period in the library so you can do some research for your paper that is due before winter break." The class is excited, and Jeremy stands to carry my bag for me again.

"I got it, Jer, but thanks." I pick up my bag, and I'm one of the first to get to the library. I pick a seat where I can be alone, though it is obvious that Jeremy wants to sit with me. I pull out my notebooks and start to work on my paper. It is almost done—okay, it is completely done. But I want to appear enthralled with it. We were each assigned a poem by Edna St. Vincent Millay; mine was "I Know I Am but Summer to Your Heart." It is intense and extremely appropriate. It starts "I know I am but summer to your heart, And not the full four seasons of the year." You could say it hit home when I read it.

After about twenty minutes of rereading my finished paper, I roam the reference section just to move around. No one is back in this part of the library, and l take advantage of the quiet. I lean back against the bookcase and close my eyes. I feel like crying and talk myself into holding it together. I hate this so much. Cooper is all I can think about. Sure, Jeremy is being so sweet, and I should be enjoying my last year in high school. But I feel trapped in my heart and stuck in my brain. I bang my head against the spines of the books and let out a sigh.

"You doing okay back here, Ms. Starr?" I snap my eyes open to find Cooper standing next to me. He is holding a clipboard in one hand and a book in the other. I close my eyes and take in as much air as my lungs will hold. I will not cry.

"Yes, Mr. Perez," I answer. He looks around, and it's obvious we are all alone.

"Are you dating Jeremy Fisher?" he asks, moving closer. I can smell his aftershave, so I inhale as much as my lungs can hold, breathing him in. He is wearing a white button-up shirt untucked, with a tan sweater vest over it; it goes perfect with the brown corduroy jacket and dark jeans—he totally is pulling off the "sexy young teacher" look.

"I'm not dating anyone, Mr. Perez." I swallow. "My boyfriend dumped me, and I am too heartbroken to move on," I say quietly. "Heard you are dating Ms. Sherman, maybe even a June wedding." Oops. I hadn't expected that all to slip out.

Cooper takes in a sharp breath like I had hurt him. I wouldn't normally be so bold, but I felt braver in a public place surrounded by all these books. I finally look up and see the pain of my words in his eyes. I want to tell him that I don't how to do this or ask him what I should do. I plead with my eyes, *"Teach me, Coop . . . teach me how to not love you anymore."*

"Maybe your boyfriend is just as heartbroken," he says closer to my face. "I bet that he is still in love with you and barely making it through each day without hearing your voice or feeling your touch." His words come out so fast I can hardly understand him. "And you have bad information if you think I'm dating Stacy Sherman. My girlfriend is busy with school right now but had hoped she would have waited for me when she gets out in May." I notice his hand is holding the shelf for support. Without my permission, I reach and touch it. Cooper's eyes are closed, and he doesn't move.

"I wish that were true," I whisper, and before I know it, his face is in front of mine. *Is he going to kiss me? Maybe yell at me?*

"I am still in love you, Ali," he mouths the words, then is gone. I stand there, stunned for a moment until I can breathe properly. Having Cooper's lips so close to mine has left me dizzy and my heart pounding. Back at my table, the world seems oblivious to my shattering experience. Jeremy slips into the chair across from me.

"You okay?" he asks. "You look like you are going to be sick."

"I think I am."

Christina drove me home from school, Jeremy following in my car, and I spent the rest of the week in bed. My stomach hurt so bad I was doubled over in pain; then my back would ache, and I wouldn't be able to get comfortable. I have never missed this much school—ever. My dad is superworried, but I know what I am sick with. Heartbreak. I couldn't help but wonder if it had anything to do with what Coop said to me in the deserted reference section. My hopes go up, then down. Up, then down again. A shattered heart can only take so much.

On Friday, Jeremy came over after school, bringing me all my homework. They were all separated into large envelopes and sealed to prevent the urge to cheat. I noticed the English envelope was the thickest. Jeremy and I sat on the couch as he filled me in on the gossip I'd missed. He confirmed what I feared—everyone assuming we were back together.

"I have really missed you this week," he tells me after we have been talking for about twenty minutes. I smile weakly. *What is the right thing to do here?*

"Yeah right," I respond because I have been anything but "miss-able." I've been a shell of myself. Jeremy moves closer and takes my hand in his, and again, I get that warm feeling.

"Your hands are freezing," he remarks, then pulls me into his chest. It feels familiar, but not right, yet he is so warm that I just allow it. "I really have missed you, Ali. More than just this week," Jeremy says closer to my ear.

"Oh," is all I can say. Jeremy doesn't say anything for a while; he just seems content to hold me.

"So did you think any more about the winter dance?" he asks. I wondered when he would bring that up.

"Oh . . . Jeremy," I stutter. "I don't think that is a good idea." He turns and faces me.

"What about as friends?" His mysterious eyes plead with mine. I can see all the days and months we spent together in those eyes.

I sigh. "Let's see how I am feeling next week." I try to buy myself some time. Jeremy moves his face and brushes his lips against mine. I gasp and jump back, feeling sweat beginning to bead at my brow. Neither of us speaks—I think I'm in shock.

"I'm sorry. That was out of line," he says, our lips still close. Gosh, I miss kissing. I debate if it is ethical to kiss Jeremy and pretend that it is Cooper.

"It's okay," I mumble, and as I say this, they touch again. "Thanks for bringing me my homework." I lean back. He runs his hands through his hair, and I stand up, Jeremy following my lead.

"Feel better, okay?" Jeremy says, bending down and kissing the top of my head before he leaves. I sit stunned on the couch for a few minutes once he is gone. When I stand, my legs are so cramped it is hard to walk, but I stumble into the kitchen to make myself some hot tea.

I take my tea and homework envelopes to my bedroom. It takes me all of two seconds to rip open the English one. Inside are just a few sheets of paper regarding my actual classwork. The remainder are handwritten notes from Cooper. They are dated starting back at the first day of school until now, which means there are almost eighty notes.

Three hours later, I am more confused than ever. Cooper's words were a mixture of love and uncertainty. He writes about how hard it is to see me every day, but how this arrangement is necessary. His last letter is the most troubling. It says:

> *If you love someone enough you should let them go. This is what I will do. I release you from feeling obligated to stick by me. Ali, it is over. Go live your life*

I read these four life-changing sentences a dozen times. I didn't know my heart could hurt any more, but it did.

I reluctantly go back to school on Monday. Everything seemed to look different, feel different. Jeremy walked me to English every day that week, and I let him hold my backpack and hand. So I'm a terrible person—I just needed some strength, and he was willing to provide it. I watched Cooper look at us every time we came in together. Hey, if he wanted me out of his life, then fine. I made a split-second decision scribbling some words on a scrap paper and tossing it on Jeremy's desk. He snatched it and read it under his desk. I watched as his eyes widen; then he smiled, writing something back.

No to the dance-yes to a date. Tonight.

Pick you up at seven.

The dance is tomorrow night, and today is the last day before our two weeks of winter vacation. I held the paper flat against my desk, not noticing the class was absolutely silent. I looked up to find Cooper standing over my desk.

"Is there something more interesting than my lecture, Ms. Starr?" His voice was strained.

"Mr. Perez, that is my paper," Jeremy said, quickly defending me.

"Then, Mr. Fisher, why is it on Allison's desk?" The way he said my name was brutal. Like a bitter taste he couldn't get out of his mouth. Our papers were due today at the start of class, and Mr. Perez spent the remainder of the class lecturing about, you know, I can't even remember. The bell rings, and the rest of the students flee before any homework can be assigned over vacation. Now it was just me, Cooper, and Jeremy in the empty classroom.

Cooper never took his eyes off me while he spoke. "Mr. Fisher, have a good vacation. Ms. Starr, I will need to speak to you regarding this behavior."

"But, Mr. Perez," Jeremy tries again. Our teacher looked at him.

"That will be all, Jeremy. Please shut the door as you leave." Jeremy gave me an apologetic look but left as he was told. I sat staring at the note on my desk, noticing how silent the room now was.

"I'm sorry"—I swallow—"Mr. Perez, about the note." He sat on the desk in front of me.

"So you are going out with that tool tonight?" I looked up into his bright blue eyes.

"I was told to go live my life," I spat and stood face-to-face with the man I still loved. "You didn't even call me on my birthday." My voice dropped. I know that he couldn't, but it still hurt. I had some expectations of celebrating my day into adulthood. I had a lot of expectations that I know will never be met, and the thought is shattering.

"I should give you detention," he said, and I felt my jaw drop open.

I felt my blush burn my face, and I moved closer. "Then do it." Cooper grabbed my face and pulled me into a fierce kiss. It was filled with anger and passion for the brief seconds it lasted. I pulled his face to mine and let a thousand memories flood me. My fingers wove through his longer hair, and all I could think was, *Finally*. When he released me, I stumbled backward, and he stood. Just looking at him, hair messed up and eyes a little wild, all I wanted to do was jump him and take him on the classroom floor.

"Don't think for one second that this has been easy for me, Ali." He swallowed, and I could see tears in his eyes. "I have wanted to hold you"— his voice low—"to kiss you, to make you happy. Just be with you every single day. It is killing me." He put his hand on his chest. "Can't you see?" Cooper bent to meet my gaze. "I will always love you." His fingers trace my cheeks and touch my neck. Our gazes lock, and I want to kiss him again. "You will always be the only one for me."

I'm too afraid to say anything, so I act on impulse and let my lips come back to his. This time the kiss is gentle and sweet, the anger gone and the true emotion of the situation remains—love. I pull my face away from his and find his eyes open. I am so overwhelmed that I just need to get out of here. It feels like the walls are closing in on us. I grab my stuff and make a beeline to the door but stop before I push it open. I turn to have one last look at Cooper.

"Coop," I choke out. He is watching me, and I can see his eyes are filled with tears. I swallow back my own emotion. "You are the only man who will ever hold my heart." My courage subsides, and I just about run to my car. I'm not surprised to find Jeremy leaning against it, waiting for me.

He walks toward me and cups my face in his hands. "Are you okay?" His face is full of concern, and I'm positive I look like a complete mess. I sure feel like one. "Did Mr. Perez . . . did he do something to you?" He holds my gaze to make sure I answer honestly.

I shake my head. "No. Of course not." I have to pause to breathe. "I'm just not used to getting into trouble." A smile pulls across Jeremy's lips.

"My little Ali Goody Two-shoes," he whispers, smirking. I sigh in relief, knowing that I just dodged a bullet. Jeremy is still holding my face and now has a strange look in his eyes. I know that look—it was the same one he had right . . . before . . .

Jeremy's mouth almost smashes into mine. His lips are eager as his hands slides from my cheeks to the back of my head. He keeps kissing my unresponsive mouth until he is satisfied. I couldn't react in time to push him back. I literally froze in shock. *Why does he think he has the right to kiss me?*

"I'll see you tonight at seven," he says, kissing me one last time before jogging to his car.

Oh yeah. Because I agreed to go out with him tonight. Jeremy thinks we are getting back together.

Eight

Cooper

I don't drink very often, but, man, right now I am pretty drunk. Ali has been out with that punk, Jeremy, three times over her winter break. What I can't wrap my mind around is how she kissed me that last day of school and went right into Jeremy's arms.

I should have given her a detention.

I walked to her house tonight and am just waiting for her to get home. I just want to see her, maybe even talk to her. The last time that *he* brought her home *he* tried to kiss her, and she almost let him. Maybe she knew I was watching because she looked around then went inside, alone, leaving Fisher on her doorstep. It was pretty sweet seeing how bad he wanted that kiss, how he expected it, and didn't get it.

Now I am sitting across the street and two houses down tying one on. This house is for sale, so no one is occupying it. I should buy it. That'll show her. Ali has been out for almost three hours again. Probably seeing some stupid movie and eating some stupid dinner. So stupidly predictable.

I am so stupid. I hang my stupid head in my hands and pull at my stupid hair.

I am drinking some sort of rum wrapped in a paper bag from the liquor store—I have become a cliché: drunken ex-boyfriend stalking the woman he loves and just can't let go. My stomach burns from the alcohol, so I stop drinking. The first smart thing I've done tonight. Leaning against the door behind me, I just stare across the street. How could I have been so hasty in breaking things off with her? I haven't forgotten one minute of our summer, though we are now plagued with the colder weather . . . colder times.

My eyes close as I picture Ali the first day I saw her: dark hair pulled up into a high ponytail and big sunglasses covering most of her face. I had been watching her for a good ten minutes before she even noticed me. Once she did, my life changed. I watched her from the water as she watched me from the sand. The night that I kissed her, six days later, was like nothing I have ever experienced before. Her body fit to mine, her lips soft but urgent.

Not like the last time I kissed her. I was so upset seeing her agree to go out with that idiot, I just couldn't think straight. I had written that letter only because I didn't want to hold her back—then to see her moving on. My emotions and testosterone just reacted. I wanted to keep on holding her and kissing her, but it isn't possible. Our relationship isn't possible. My heart hurts so bad I am physically in pain.

No. Wait. That would be the rum.

I lean over the porch and throw up the only thing in my stomach, alcohol. I all but curl up in a ball and cry. What the hell, I do end up curling up and let the pain have me . . . then pass out.

I wake up and feel something soft over me and know someone is close by. I try to sit up and see that Ali is next to me reading a book with a flashlight. She notices that I am awake.

"You almost got caught out here," she says, putting her book down and turning the flashlight off. There is a blanket over me, and I recognize it as the quilt from her bed that we had lain on back in September. I try to sit all the way up and am immediately too dizzy and want to puke again. Ali shifts and fumbles with something next to her.

"Here," she says, helping me. "I have water and crackers for you." Ali's arms slip under mine as she props me against the wall. She is so close to me, taking care of me. I can smell the coconut scent surrounding her, and the sense of being home surrounds my heart.

"How did you know I was here?" I ask, taking the water and sipping it. A grin crosses her lips.

"I've seen you out here every night that I've gone out with Jeremy," she mumbles. "When he dropped me off, I noticed you slouched over and waited until he left to come over. When I found you, well, I guess I knew you could use some help."

I rub my head. "What time is it?" The moon hangs lazily in the sky. I think, or hope, I have thrown up most of the alcohol I consumed, but I am still feeling the effects.

"Three in the morning," she answers.

"It's not what you think," I say, feeling my stomach roll. Ali nods, watching me.

"What is it then, Cooper?" Her eyes look as sad as I feel. I want to tell her that I just can't let her go and how much I love her. But I am buzzed, and when I tell her how I really feel, I know I need to be sober so she takes me seriously.

Instead I say, "I don't know." She hands me another bottle of water, more crackers, and a couple of sticks of gum. Oh, man. I so suck right now.

"Can you walk?" she demands suddenly.

"You're right." I push to stand and immediately curse the invention of rum. "I need to get home." Ali shakes her head and sighs loudly, balancing my weight with her shoulders.

"You live too far away to walk, and I'm not letting you in my car if you're just going to throw up again," she says, struggling to lead me forward. I make a mental note to ask her how she knows where I live. "My dad is fighting a fire in the farmlands up north and won't be home for three, maybe four more, days. You can crash at my place, but just for the night."

I know that I should be saying no and walking home, but I can't. "I'm drunk," I state the obvious. Ali laughs and pulls me forward. I am vaguely aware that she somehow managed to get me upstairs and has tucked me into her bed. I can feel her pulling my shoes off and her hesitation as she considers what to do with the rest of my clothes. My eyes are closed, and she is humming while placing extra blankets on me. The room is spinning, and I want to make it stop.

"You are freezing," she says to herself, thinking I have passed out again. She sits on the bed and brushes the hair from my face. "You are so handsome, Cooper." Her lips press softly to my forehead. "I miss you every day, and every day I wish that things could be different. Why did you write that last letter, huh? What made you think that would make anything better?" she whispers then leaves the room. I ache at the thought of her leaving. I miss her too, and I want to tell her, but the rum has rendered me mute. Slowly my mind drifts into a disturbed sleep.

What a horrible night. My head hurts more than I ever thought possible; now that I think about it, so does the rest of me. I roll over and feel the tightness of my empty stomach. I need to eat. I swing my feet out of bed and realize I am still in my clothes from yesterday. I don't even remember how I got home. I force my eyes open, trying to pull back what memory I have from last night. I wanted to talk to Allison, so I decided to walk to her house, and on the way was a liquor store . . . I bought a bottle of rum . . . Ali was on a date, so I camped out across the street . . . oh shit.

My head snaps up, and I force my eyes open. I'm in Ali's room. Ali found me last night and took care of me. I look around the room that is decorated in mostly pinks and yellow. I am trying to reconstruct the events from last night. I hope I haven't made things worse between us. There is a note on the pillow:

Cooper, sleep as long as you'd like. I put a fresh towel in the bathroom so you can shower. My dad is taller than you, but I found something that might fit you.

I groan in embarrassment and look at the clock. It is almost noon. I pull myself to my feet and make it to the bathroom. I strip off my clothes and turn on the hot water. The shower feels good but not good enough to make me feel better. After I towel off, I pull on Mr. Starr's clothes—jeans are a little long and big, so is the shirt, but they will do. I find and use Ali's toothbrush; that will be my little secret. I step back into the bedroom and inhale. It smells like Ali. I want to look and touch everything, but I hear noise downstairs. She must know I am up. Time for the walk of shame.

I make my way quietly into the kitchen. Ali has earbuds in and is humming and swaying to the music that I can't hear. There is a pot of coffee brewing, and she is making pancakes. I lean against the counter and just watch her. It looks like it will start to rain any second, but the dim early afternoon light seems to dance off her like the summer sun. Her hips are slowly moving back and forth; her hair is hanging down to the middle of her back. She is wearing sweatpants and a tank top. She is the most beautiful person I have ever seen.

I can't take it anymore. I don't care about how stupid and drunk I was last night. I don't care that I told her to move on. All I care about is her, Allison. I love her and need to be close to her. I move across the cold kitchen floor and put my hand on her swaying hips. Ali jumps and lets out a little scream.

I remove the earbuds as she turns around. "It's just me," I say, smiling. "Who did you expect?"

Ali swallows and turns back to the stove. "I am making you pancakes," she says evenly. I guess that is fair. My feelings have only grown stronger—I can't expect hers to be the same especially since I told her to move on. Oh, and that stupid jerk, Jeremy. I pull my hand back, but she stops me, putting it back on her hip. "How are you feeling?" Her voice is now soothing and concerned, and it takes me a moment to answer because her skin is exposed between her pants and shirt, and I want to touch it.

"Better, thanks to you," I say, moving so my front is almost pressing to her back. I lean in and inhale her scent. I just want to hold her tight. "If I said anything last night . . ."

Ali laughs at me, not with me because I am too ashamed to laugh. "You were pretty messed up." She puts the last of the pancakes on a plate and turns off the burner. "I couldn't just leave you there." She turns around, and my hands seem glued to where she has placed them. "You keep showing up, and I don't know what to do anymore." She puts the palms of her hands on my chest, and I wait, expecting her to push me away.

"I'm sorry," I whisper. Thunder interrupts us, and Ali jumps. My arms instinctively wrap around her, protecting her from any harm. Rain lightly falls outside, and we are standing there holding each other, unable to make eye contact.

"Why are you sorry?" Ali asks. I snort out a laugh.

"I am sorry for so many things I don't know where to start," I admit. Ali looks up with her big brown doe eyes.

"I don't like Jeremy," she says, to my surprise. "I just want to feel wanted." Her cheeks blush, and I can tell she wants to look away. I hold her face with my hands so she can't. I've missed this face too much to not have the opportunity to stare at it.

"You have always been wanted, Ali," I say with so much passion I can't think straight. My lips are almost on hers. "Sometimes we can't have what we want the most." Ali closes her eyes and takes in a long breath. I know her well enough to know this is what she does before she makes a decision or before she says something important.

When her eyes open again, they are smoldering. "If it is me that you want, Coop"—she pauses and runs her hands under my borrowed shirt—"you can have me." I anticipated her to tell me to leave, that I've hurt her too much. I want her so bad that I lay awake at night regretting that I would never have a chance to even touch her again, and here she is, offering herself to me. I pull her against me hard, and our mouths almost slam together.

Ali lets out a small groan that almost stops my heart. We are kissing, and our hands are everywhere. I open my eyes and find hers open as well, but nothing stops. It almost ignites more in us. She is breathing hard, and I'm not sure how she managed it, but she has my shirt off. This reminds me of our last night on the beach. Ali leans back and runs her hands over my chest; my knees buckle. She tumbles on top of me, and we land on her kitchen floor, which makes us both burst into laughter.

We are lying side by side, laughing and catching our breath. I don't know what to do. I want to be with this girl in every sense, but I am still her teacher. The conflict that battles inside of me is torture. It doesn't help when Ali sits up and her tank top has been flung beside us. I can't look away even if I wanted to. She is wearing a black lace bra, which contrasts with the pale skin it's covering, and it fills my vision. Ali gathers her hair in a loose ponytail and leans over me and traces my lips with the tip of her tongue. I am paralyzed.

She slides back on top of me, pressing her warm soft body against my chest as she begins to kiss me slowly, hesitantly. My fingers knot themselves in her hair, holding her face to mine with one hand, the other resting on her hip again. Ali shifts her weight back and forth, and I momentarily forget how to breathe. I realize what she is doing, and it is too late. She has slipped her sweatpants off, and I can't breathe at the sight of her matching panties. Her mouth assaults mine, and I can hear my throaty groan.

"Ali," I whisper, trying to find the will to stop. Of course, stopping is the last thing that I want to do. I want to take her in my arms and hold her forever. I want our first time to be romantic and special, not on the kitchen floor.

She can feel my hesitation and leans back. "I thought that this is what you wanted." Her face flushes. Of course I want this, how could I not? I can see her starting to fall apart waiting for me to tell her no again. I sit up and pull her close and hold her tight.

"It is," I say into her hair. "It is, Ali—gosh. There isn't anything I want more than you." I can feel her beginning to relax. My fingers are exploring the newly exposed skin which is causing goose bumps to rise on her. I help her to her feet and led her into the living room where I wrap a blanket around her shoulders.

Immediately we are both back on the beach, a bonfire burning bright behind us, a thousand stars sparkling overhead. As I did before, using the blanket, I pull Allison closer to me and tilt her face toward mine. I become completely saturated with love for the girl I feel like I could drown. Her eyes are wide and blazing with desire. My will is shot, and I give in to her and to myself. I have been away from her intimacy for months, and I can't take it for another second.

I think she is surprised when I pull her face to mine, and just like on the beach, the blanket falls silently to the floor. Ali's slender arms wrap around my neck, and I easily lift her off the floor. The couch isn't far, so I make the short walk, not breaking our kiss, and gently lay her down. I position myself over her delicate body, not letting her feel any of my weight, but Ali pulls me down, so we are pressed together. Her fingers lace themselves in my hair, and she groans softly as I kiss her neck.

"I love you," I whisper in her ear, and she trembles under me. When we make eye contact again, we both know that nothing will stop us from this moment and that nothing will interrupt us.

That is when the phone rings and interrupts us. I fall off the couch and crash to the floor. Allison jumps up, pulling the blanket off the floor to cover her exposed skin. The answering machine picks up the missed call.

"Hey, Ali," Jeremy's voice fills the room. "Just making sure we are on for tonight. Call me back . . . love ya." Ali walks over to the machine and presses a few buttons until the message is deleted. When she turns back to face me, she looks upset. I want to go to her, but it dawns on me that she might want to go on a date even if it's not with me—even if it's with a guy she claims she doesn't like.

I would be lying if I said my ego wasn't bruised. "He loves ya, huh?" Here we are, rolling around half naked and a . . . a suitor is literally calling on her.

Ali blushes and shrugs. "He says he does."

I swallow. "And what do you say back?" Ali turns around and pulls the blanket tighter around her almost-nude body.

"Nothing." Her voice is low. "I say nothing to him because that is what I feel toward him." I am washed with relief at her words. I walk across the room and take Ali in my arms.

"We just have to be patient," I tell her, kissing her head. "Can you wait for me?" I ask softly, knowing that I'd wait a lifetime for her. Ali nods slowly, looking as frustrated as I feel.

"Until May?" she asks me, leaning back. I kiss the tip of her nose. I find it ironic that I am the one asking her to wait for me when the roles are usually reversed. I'm not complaining. I like the fact that this smoking-hot chick is trying to take advantage of me.

"Until May, then we can be together all the time." Ali smiles that smile I love best and leans in to press her lips to mine.

"And then forever," she repeats back to me. We sat on her kitchen floor listening to the rain, holding each other; love and patience seeped through us. There was nothing more we needed to say.

May. Only five more months. One hundred and fifty days of cold showers.

Nine

Allison

Cooper and I are back on track, or the best we can be, and have been talking every day for hours. We have hatched a plan, a secret schedule to be able to still be close. He even snuck over once while my dad was at work. On Christmas we exchanged gifts. I gave him a new watch, and he gave me a necklace with a seashell on it. He said it was from our beach and has had it with him since our last night there. I wear it every day instead of the key bracelet. I couldn't wear it with Christina knowing what it meant to me. I want to take things to the next level with him, but understand why we can't. Five months—that is my focus—just five more ridiculously long months.

It is January and our first day back to school from winter break. I am actually looking forward to my English class today. I know Cooper and I need to keep this secret, but he is just so incredibly handsome, and I can spend the entire class period ogling him instead of ignoring him. I hope I can keep myself under control. It won't be easy since when I left for winter break, I was always a sneeze away from tears, and now you can't wipe the smile off my face. I am walking between second and third period when Jeremy approaches me.

"So, you never called me back last night," he says, putting his arm around my shoulders. I want to shrug off his arm but also don't want to hurt his feelings or burn my friendship bridge with him. He has been so sweet to me, even after I called him back the day Cooper heard his message.

I told him that I liked spending time with him, but I just didn't feel the same way. He said he understood and asked if we could still hang out. I reluctantly agreed and saw him one more time over the break, where he tried to kiss me. Since then I have been trying to avoid him, unsuccessfully.

"I'm sorry about that. I was just busy," I lamely explain. He leans in and kisses my cheek.

"Can I take you out tonight?" he asks optimistically. "As friends?" As if adding the friends is going to change how he really feels about me. Sorry, buddy, not this girl.

"I really need to focus on school right now," I lie. He takes in the information I feed him and nods, knowing my nerdy background.

"Okay," he says easily. "See you in English." He kisses me lightly on the cheek once more. I watch him disappear into the sea of students. I walk into third period dazed.

"Oh, Allison," Mr. Thorn calls as I take my seat. "They need you in the office, something about tutoring. Here is a pass." He hands me a slip of paper, and I look at it confused. Do they know something? Fear fills me, and sweat covers my skin. I swallow and smile.

"Thank you, Mr. Thorn," I manage to say as I turn and walk out of class. I stop first in the girls' restroom. I need to make sure I look innocent and pulled together. I do look paler than usual. After standing in front of the mirror for ten minutes, I will some color to my face, or so I convince myself. I take the slowest route to the office and find my counselor on the phone. She motions for me to sit, so I do.

"Hello, Allison," she greets me. She seems calm, which is good. Of course if I were in some sort of trouble, I would have been called to the principal's office, not the guidance counselor's.

"Hello, Mrs. Brown. What's up?" I am shaking. She is holding a folder and hands it to me.

"This is a list of all the seniors who say they have been taking tutoring with you and Mr. Perez. I need for you to sort it and mark their progress. I think some of them are lying about showing up at all. You know how it is. I have a desk here for you," she said as she walked me a short distance and set me up. I let out the air I have been holding in my lungs and opened the folder. I'm paranoid.

Just like she had said, the progress that Mr. Perez had kept of the students we have seen since September. I spent third and fourth period in the office doing my paperwork, which is good because then I don't have to watch Ms. Sherman bounce around for an hour. The bell rings for lunch, and I start to pack my things. I just needed to turn in what I found to Mrs. Brown but got distracted as Cooper entered the office.

I wanted to wave to him but knew better. He didn't see me anyway. He looked concerned and went into Mr. Matthew's office, the principal, running his hand through his hair. I let myself move a little closer since the door didn't close all the way. I don't usually eavesdrop, but today it seemed appropriate, so I pretended to still be looking at my tutoring folder. No one was in the office except a secretary who was too busy on the phone to even notice me.

"It has been brought to my attention, Mr. Perez, that you might have some special interest in a student here at Chino Prep," Mr. Matthew said.

There was a pause. "No special or any interest at all, sir," Cooper answered. I held my breath listening. "Who would say such a thing?"

"It was noted that you spend extra time with Allison Starr," Matthew countered.

"Well, of course I do, sir, she is the senior English tutor. We work together three times a week with her classmates." Cooper sounded so sure and confident. "It is anything but special attention, sir. This obligation was passed to me by Mr. Snyder. I didn't choose it."

"Well, she *is* a good-looking girl and you are young," he tested him. Cooper laughed, but I could tell he was uncomfortable.

"Mr. Matthew, I can assure you I have absolutely no interest whatsoever in Allison Starr." Cooper cleared his throat. "I have suspected that she may have a crush on me, but my feelings have always and will always be strictly professional. I would never look at a student that way, sir. And you may not know this, but Stacy Sherman and I are seeing each other." He paused. "It isn't serious, but we have been out a few times." He has to be convincing, I tell myself. Lying, that is what he is doing. Has to be.

"Good to hear, Cooper," the principal says. "Students may have their ideas and rumors, so we must keep ourselves professional."

"Yes, sir. I find most students, Allison, for example, may be immature and deluded with wild ideas. She really is nothing more than a student to me." My heart is pounding hard in my chest, and my stomach is in a torturing knot. "You understand how students can be. Sometimes they become delusional and talk themselves into such an infatuation that they begin to believe it to be true. Allison is a good student, sir, but I again assure you she is nothing more than a student to me."

"Very well—glad we cleared that all up," the principal says, and they shake hands. I am frozen against the wall when Cooper leaves. He doesn't see me or know that I heard him call me immature, delusional, and infatuated. Oh. And the best part—the girlfriend. Sure, he was just saying that to throw Mr. Matthew off, but gosh, he sounded so sure and convincing. I had to wonder, had he been lying to the principal or to me?

I sit through sixth period with Christina, and she is telling me about this new guy she likes, Andrew. I want to tell her everything about Cooper, but she thinks things ended months ago. I feel like I am going to throw up. There is an ache in my lower back, and it feels like someone has kicked me there repeatedly. The bell rings. I stand and move robotically. My world has shifted and is crumbling before my very eyes. I am aware that Jeremy is walking me to class, holding my bag. I take my seat and try to fight back the urge to vomit.

I hear Cooper call the class to order. He is talking about winter break and what some of the students did. I didn't hear him call my name.

"Hey, Ali." Jeremy touches my hand. I look at him, and his eyes widen. "You okay?" I stand up and realize everyone is staring at me. I close my eyes and feel so dizzy and brace myself against the desk. I finally will my eyes to open so I don't throw up in class, and Cooper is staring at me. I watch him take a step toward me, his eyebrows knit together in worry, and his hand raises then falls back to his side. The tears burn in my eyes, and I just head for the door, not looking back.

"Allison," Cooper calls my name.

"I will take care of this, Mr. P.," Jeremy says, following me out. I am only a few feet outside of class when Jeremy catches up with me. I wanted to run except my legs feel like they are filled with lead.

"Hey," Jeremy says, holding my shoulders. "What is going on? Do you need me to take you to the nurse?" His voice is low and gentle.

"I'm fine," I lie, panting for air.

"Like hell you are," he says, taking me into his arms. Maybe this is where I belong, with someone like Jeremy, someone at my maturity level that I can be infatuated with. I gulp in the air, but it never seems like enough. The words Coop said to the principal echo in my head.

"I'm not feeling well—I just needed some fresh air," I tell him. He accepts this answer and sits with me until class is almost over. He keeps his arms around me, and I hold back the tears. Jeremy doesn't ask me anything; he just lets me be. We are still sitting on a stone planter as Cooper walks up.

"Everything okay out here?" the two-timing son of a gun asks. I can't even look at him.

"I think so, Mr. Perez, we were just coming back to class," Jeremy answers and helps me to my feet. I see Cooper's hand twitch as if he wants to help me again.

"Very well," he says, and Jeremy leads me to my seat. The minutes tick by until the bell finally rings.

"Can I take you home?" Jeremy asks.

I shake my head no. "I am staying late for some tutoring stuff," I tell him. I am supposed to go over the discrepancies I found earlier today. Cooper is sitting on the edge of his desk talking to Hillary, who is obviously flirting with him. She is sticking out her chest and flipping her hair. Cooper doesn't seem to notice any of it. *Just another delusional teenager. Maybe I'll start a club. Or maybe he can date her too; add a third to the mix.* All her questions are finally answered, and we are alone. Since the class is empty, I stand up. I feel like I am going to pass out but push myself to take a step further on my uncooperative legs.

Before I can reach the door Cooper shuts it and turns around; concern is covering his face. "Please tell me what is wrong," he begs, opening his arms as he walks toward me.

"I can't even talk to you right now," I manage to say. I gather all the strength I have and try to move past him. Cooper grabs me by the shoulders, and my heart rate doubles. His eyes are a dark blue, like stormy water.

"Come on, Ali, it's me here." He looks so upset, but I still shake him off. Not again. I can't go through not having him again. I need to be strong and stand up for myself.

"No, it isn't, Mr. Perez. I would hate to ruin our professional relationship with my immaturity and be deluded into thinking this was something more." I drop my bag on the ground. "You know, since I am so delusional with infatuation and all. Oh, and what would the woman you've been dating think of all of this, Ms. Sherman? Bet she'd get real upset to find us alone in your classroom." I put my hands on my hips and wait for his rebuttal.

He looks stunned. "Let me explain."

Then I do the unthinkable—I slap him. Really hard. Cooper's hand flies to his cheek, and I push past him.

My skin is so clammy that I feel extremely cold as I walk outside. I don't know where to go or what to do. I just want to get away. The courtyard is deserted, and I spin around. The ground seems to be uneven under my feet, as if I am walking on a boat. It is hard to catch my breath, and the pain in my stomach is so intense I feel dizzy. The pain in my heart is even worse. I look around for somewhere to sit, but my legs won't move—they are numb.

My world starts to spin, and I can't focus on anything. Black spots cloud my vision. It feels like I am being strangled. The last thing I remember seeing is Cooper running toward me, but he is sideways, and I hear him yelling my name, but he sounds like he is under water. My body crashed into the hard cold cement.

Nothing except total darkness.

Ten

Cooper

It is obvious Ali heard what I told Mr. Matthews. What did she expect? That I confess how much I love her and risk everything? I mean, when I found Chino on the map, its largest landmark was the Men's Prison. She just slapped me, and I have to admit, for someone so small, it hurt like hell. She looked really messed up though. Her skin was paler than normal, and she seemed to be walking funny. I bend down and pick her bag up off the ground and go outside; she can't be too far, and I have to explain.

She is still in the courtyard outside my classroom. She is not moving right, rigid, as if she is in pain. I call to her, and she doesn't respond. I move toward her, feeling nervous. Something is definitely wrong.

Then she turns and looks at me, her eyes roll back into her head, and she crashes to the ground.

"Allison!" I yell and get to her just as she hits the concrete. Her skin is clammy and turning blue.

"Help!" I yell, scooping her head into my hands. I keep yelling and try to take her pulse. It is very weak. After what seemed like days of yelling, some goth-looking kid appears.

"What happened?" he asks, looking strung out and unconcerned.

"Call 911," I demand, looking and pointing at the cell phone in his hand. I turn back to Ali and try to decide if I should start CPR.

"I did call, when I saw her fall," he says slowly. I turn Ali and lay her flat on her back, keeping my fingers on her carotid artery.

I lean in closer to listen for breaths hovering my ear right above her mouth. Her breathing is so shallow I can hardly feel it. "Ali, listen to me," I tell her. "I need you to be okay. I need you to fight." This can't be happening.

I can hear the sirens but can't tell how close they are. A fog of fear has engulfed me. Out of thin air, a team of paramedics is around us. One of them is pulling me back, away from Ali.

"Sir, can you tell us what happened?" some guy starts asking me. I watch as they lift her to a gurney and put an oxygen mask over her face.

"She was acting strange . . . she fell . . . passed out," I tried to explain. "I need to stay with her." I moved forward.

"Sir, we will take good care of her. Can you give us some more information?" I pushed the oh-so-helpful paramedic aside, but he stopped me. "You said she had been acting strange, can you elaborate?"

"I will tell you whatever you want on the ride over." I head toward the ambulance, not letting Allison out of my sight. They don't fight me anymore. Someone continues to ask me questions, and I give them one-word answers. All my attention is on the fragile girl strapped to the gurney.

I sit next to Ali and take her cold hand in mine. Her eyes keep flickering open, but she is unaware. I want her to know I am here and not to be afraid. The paramedics are putting all kinds of bands on her and cut her shirt open and stick something to her chest. When her heart rate shows on the monitor, I hear them talk about problems. I am just watching for Ali's dark eyes to open.

"I'm here, Ali." I lean in and whisper into her ear. Her skin is so cold and almost chalky. Her eyes finally look in my direction. "I am here," I say again and move as close as I can. "I love you." Her eyes roll back, and then the monitor makes a horrible beeping sound. I turn to look at it.

There was no rhythm. Ali's heart had stopped beating. I broke Allison Starr's heart.

***

Time doesn't mean anything to me anymore. Everything around me was a blur of noise and movement. When we arrived at the emergency room, everyone, except me, was in "fast forward" as the paramedics rushed Ali somewhere deep into the hospital. I was taken somewhere else to answer questions. Reviewing my brief answers in the ambulance ride, I was told they needed even more information. After telling them who I was, her teacher, and what I had seen, her passing out, they called her father and I called her Aunt Trudy.

"Hello," she answered cheerfully.

"Trudy," I managed to say.

"Who is this?" She sounded instantly concerned.

"It's Ryan." I held back a sob. "Cooper Ryan, and something is wrong with Ali." I gave her a run of the events, as much as I could.

"I'm on my way," she said, and the line went dead.

I kept asking about Ali at the nurses' desk, but because I wasn't family, I wasn't given any information.

"Sir, I know you are her teacher and are concerned, but . . ."

"I'm not her teacher!" I yell at the nurse. "I'm her boyfriend." The admitting nurse's eyes widen then squint.

"According to the paperwork, you said you are her English teacher." I can't remember filling out any paperwork. "Which is it, Mr. Perez?" I don't answer. I just stumble back and somehow make it to a chair.

The hospital clock ticks by, but I don't have any idea how long I have been here.

"Where is she?" a deep voice booms. "I'm her father, Robert Starr." I jump to my feet and walk boldly over to him. The nurse is explaining something to him, and fear inflicts his face. Sometime on my short walk over to him, I started to cry.

"Mr. Starr," I stutter. He looks down to me, and his eyes are troubled and rimmed with tears. "I'm Cooper," I say. He stares at me for a long minute.

"You brought her, my Ali, here?" he says. "The teacher?" I don't know how to answer him. Before I can answer, he asks, "Hold on . . . Cooper . . . from the beach this past summer?"

I sigh and look to the shiny white hospital floor. "Yes," is all I can manage, answering both questions. I swallow, waiting to be punched or yelled at.

Neither happens.

Mr. Starr pulls me into a hug and starts to cry. Not just cry, but full-on sobbing. My barrier cracks, and I cry along with him. My whole being feels like it is crumbling as I embrace him back. He finally pulls it together long enough to have it all click in his head.

He pushes me back, and the understanding is just beneath the surface of his glare. "Wait." I hold my breath. "Ali's boyfriend or her teacher?"

"Sir," I say. "I can explain." Before I can, Mr. Starr's fist comes in contact with my face like I had first anticipated. I stumble backward and crumple to the cold floor.

***

I hear voices and want to open my eyes, but one seems to be swollen shut. My head is splitting with pain, and my whole face hurts. I decide to try to hear what the whispers are saying.

"No, Robert, you listen to me. Ali met him at the beach this summer. She had no clue that he would end up being her teacher." It was Trudy. She was defending me to Allison's dad, Robert.

"But he is her teacher," Mr. Starr huffed.

"So you knock him out cold even though it is because of him your daughter is still alive?" Silence. "I know this boy, and he loves Allison, teacher or not." A cold hand pressed against my forehead. I tried to open my eyes.

"Allison," I gurgled out and tried to sit up.

"Whoa, Ryan," Trudy says, supporting me in sitting up.

Panic rippled though me. "Allison," I try again. No one spoke, so I try to open my eyes. I could see Mr. Starr holding his head in his hands, leaning against the wall.

"She is stable for now," her aunt tells me. *For now . . . what does that mean?*

"What happened?" I began to shake. Trudy looked over to Ali's father who in turn looked at me.

"Aortic aneurysm," he answered dully. What is that? Trudy was gently patting my back as he continued. "The walls of her heart are weak . . . like her mother's." Mr. Starr's cheeks were wet as tears continued to stream from his eyes. "Allison's hasn't burst, so she still has a chance."

"What can I do?" *No, this can't be happening. Not Ali. This isn't right.* Mr. Starr lifted his head from his hands and stared into my eyes. He seemed to evaluate me before he walked toward me. I flinched and expected to be knocked out cold again. He is a huge man, and I'm sure the next blow could kill me.

"From what her doctor told me, because of you she is still alive, by getting her here so quickly." He put his hand on my shoulder. "Thank you, Cooper." He squeezed my shoulder. It felt like we now had an unspoken understanding. I'm not your typical man's man who after another guy punches you feels better and puts a misunderstanding aside. No, I'm the let's-talk-it-out kind of guy and feel like Mr. Starr and I should discuss this further.

"Mr. Starr," a man in a white doctor's coat approached us. "You can see her now." Trudy helped me get to my feet and steady me as we moved forward. "Sorry, son, the ICU is restricted to family only."

Mr. Starr stepped up. "He is family," he simply stated and put an arm around me. I'm not sure how long ago this guy had punched me, but I'm now family. Maybe I need to reconsider learning how to throw a punch and talk a little less. It does seem to speed up the process of being comrades.

The doctor didn't question Robert and led us back into a sectioned-off area of the hospital. It was explained that we could go in one at a time. Mr. Starr went in first, leaning over her bed. He spoke to her softly and took her hand. He lifted her hand to his face and began to cry again. It was a horrible scene to watch.

Trudy let out a long sigh, and I turned to look at her. "She needs to have surgery." I looked at her. "It is very risky but necessary."

"I can't lose her," I tell Trudy. "I love her." She just nods and takes my hand, and we just wait for our turn. Trudy lets me go in before she does.

Ali looks so small and fragile in that hospital bed. Her breathing sounds constricted, and the monitor beeps in an unsteady rhythm. I sit in the hard plastic chair next to the bed and take her cold hand in mine.

"I don't know if you can hear me, Ali, but I am here, and I'm not going anywhere." I kiss her hand. "I love you, and you have to pull through. I'll do anything." As I say the words, it all seems to make sense in my head. Everything is now clear. The fog that had engulfed me has vanished next to Ali. She is like the sun to me, burning away the confusing haze. I make up my mind and know what must be done. I sit with her until my time is up, telling her my plan, then quickly explain to Trudy what I am going to do.

Once outside I realize I don't have a car. So I pull out my cell phone and making one of the many calls I'll make today. It rings three times before there is an answer.

"This is Principal Matthews," my boss answers. I take a deep breath and can feel that I am making the right decision.

"Mr. Matthews," I say steadily, "this is Cooper Perez."

"Cooper, is everything all right?"

"Sir, I am sorry, but due to a family emergency I need to resign my position." There is silence on his end.

"Are you telling me you're quitting?"

"Yes." I say it direct and with no other explanation.

"I heard that Allison Starr was in some sort of accident. Does that have anything to do with this?"

I let out a sigh. "No disrespect, but since I just quit, I don't have to answer any more questions."

"If I find out you lied about your relationship regarding a student . . ." His voice trails off with his threat.

"Understood," I snap back. "You'll have my letter of resignation first thing tomorrow." I hang up and call my lawyer.

I quickly inform him of the entire situation—from start to finish. He assures me that because Allison and I broke up upon realization of our situation, I am protected, and any lawsuit would be swatted down before it could ever develop. As a precaution, a lawyer from his staff will contact the school and smooth over everything and make sure there are no misunderstandings. I want all my bases covered, so I ask him a few things about quitting my job. Some things mean more to me than a paycheck.

Once that phone call is finished, I call my mom. I get her voice mail and spout out the bare bones of what is happening. My mom is understanding, but in this situation, I can't see her being . . . supportive. This job meant a lot to her, almost as much as it had meant to me. But she met Allison and knew I'd do anything for her, so I don't think she'll be surprised.

I make one more call before I go back into the ICU waiting area. It is to my estate lawyer. I explain to him what I am planning on doing next and what I need from him. Naturally he has some questions, but when he is clear of the seriousness of the events at hand, he complies. Now is the hardest part.

I have to talk to Mr. Starr and hope he understands. I wish I knew how to block punches.

Eleven

Allison

The last thing I can remember is Cooper holding my hand, telling me he loved me. I can't open my eyes because they are so heavy, but I still try to force them. My chest feels like I have been running as fast as I could for about ten days in a row without a break. It hurts so badly that I open my eyes to make sure there isn't a weight of some kind pressing on my chest . . . like an elephant or something.

Now that my eyes are open, I realize that I don't know where I am, and I'm scared.

There is a mask over my mouth and wires all over my body. I struggle to move, now in full panic mode, trying to rip everything off me.

"Whoa," a gentle voice says, taking my hands in his and lightly pressing me back down into the bed. "You are okay," he says, touching my hair. "You are in the hospital. There is a problem with your heart, but they are going to fix it." I am having a hard time focusing and can't find his face, but I'd know that voice anywhere.

"What happened," I think I say. Finally Cooper moves his face into my direct line of vision. The lights overhead surround him, and he looks like he is glowing. An angel . . . my angel.

"Don't worry about that now, sweetheart," he whispers and kisses my head. "You just have to fight through this, okay? I need you to know I am here and am not leaving no matter what." I just stare at him. I can tell that he has been crying because his eyes are puffy. And one is black and blue and almost swollen shut.

"Your eye." I want to touch his face. Cooper smiles and looks down.

"I met your dad." He laughs.

"He . . . he hit you?" I can't believe this. Details are starting to come into focus. I told Dad about Cooper . . . I was at school when I collapsed with my teacher . . . Cooper rode to the hospital with me. *Oh crap. The cat is out of the bag.*

"Yeah," he answers, touching his cheek, and winces. "It is okay, I think, I mean between me and your dad. I think Trudy came to my rescue while I was out cold." There is so much to process. I feel so tired but don't want to close my eyes and lose Cooper.

"What now?" I sigh, and my chest tightens. Cooper's fingers touch my hair and then my cheek.

"You rest and get stronger so the doctor can patch you back up," he tells me.

"With us? What happens now with us?" Cooper smiles and leans in closer to me. There are so many wires attached to me I can't move. I feel his lips press against my forehead.

"Well, I was thinking about that . . . about taking things to the next level," he states. Next level, what does he mean? He must have seen the confusion in my eyes, so he continues. "I made a few calls . . ."

"How long has she been lucid?" A nurse comes into the room abruptly. Cooper keeps his eyes on mine as he answers her.

"Just a couple of minutes, ma'am," he answers.

"And what part of 'if she wakes up, buzz us immediately' didn't you understand?" Cooper leans down and kisses my forehead.

"I love you, Allison Starr," he tells me, ignoring the nurse. "I need to let this very nice woman examine you, but when she is done, there is something that I need to ask you." Then he kisses me once more and leaves the room. The nurse comes to my bedside while checking some things on my chart and the many monitors and bags attached to me.

"The doctor will be in soon with your father," she says and leaves. I take in my surroundings as best I can. I am in a glass box and attached to a hospital bed. Outside I can see my dad, Cooper, and Aunt Trudy next to the nurses' station. They are all standing around a doctor who seems to be explaining something to them. They all nod at the same time, and the doctor keeps talking using hand motions to get his point across. Cooper looks across the room and directly into my eyes. His gaze pulls me in, and he is all I can see. Right now, we are in our own private world even though we are separated by a glass wall and twenty feet.

I notice the doctor leaving the group and heading toward my door. I watch as Cooper touches my dad's arm and says something to him. Whatever he says, Cooper has my dad's full attention.

"Hello, Allison," the doctor greets me. "I was just talking to your father and family . . ." He keeps on talking, but I am watching my dad and Cooper. I can hear the doctor say something about an aneurysm, but what is going on outside my room is much more important. I can see my dad's face turn bright red, but not surprised at whatever Cooper is saying to him.

Cooper keeps talking, and my dad looks furious or scared. He looks toward me, and his eyes soften. Trudy has a small smile on her lips due to whatever the conversation is about. My dad shakes his head, and Cooper covers his heart with his hand and looks like he is pleading.

"So by this time tomorrow if you stay stable, we should have you in surgery." The doctor pats my arm.

"Surgery." I finally look at the doctor and thinking that maybe what he was saying was important too. He nods like I am supposed to understand. He makes some notes on my chart and leaves. I turn my attention back to the show outside my room. Dad and Cooper are deep in conversation.

Cooper is still talking, and my dad is listening; he doesn't look thrilled, but he doesn't look upset anymore. He seems to be deep in thought. They talk for about ten more minutes before my dad stands up and heads toward my room.

"Hey, baby girl," he says quietly.

"Hi, Daddy," I respond, and he takes my hands. "So I see you've met Cooper." My dad nods and sighs.

"Yeah," he says slowly, "we should talk about that, but when you are feeling better."

"I didn't know that he was going to be my teacher . . . I met him before that . . . we broke up." My words spilled out, and I could hear my heart monitor beeping more frequently. "I love him, Daddy."

"Calm down, honey," he said softly. "I'm not upset anymore." His smile was conflicted. "I've had the last day to get to know him, and he is a decent guy—not that any guy is ever going to be good enough for my Ali-Oops."

The last day? "How long have I been in here?"

"Thirty hours," Dad answered sadly. "The wall of your heart is weak, just like your mom's had been. If Cooper hadn't been with you . . ." We didn't say anything for a while, we didn't have to. Before my mom had died, they thought they had caught the problem in time. They didn't. I am in the same situation she was in ten years ago. "The doctor says your heart appears to have been weak for some time. Had you been experiencing any of the symptoms that you know you should be looking for?"

I would be lying if I told him no. After my mom died, we learned that this could be a genetic disease and what symptoms to look for. They include abdominal and back pain, leg pain or numbness, feelings of stress, nausea, anxiety, and rapid heart rate. I had felt most of these, and I should have seen the signs, but I just thought it was all because of my metaphoric broken heart.

"It will be okay, Dad," I tried to assure him and ignored the question he asked.

"I was so lucky to have your mother." He sounded wistful. "She was the most beautiful woman that I had ever seen, and when she agreed to marry me, I didn't think life could get any better. Then she told me she was pregnant." He paused. "Life got better." Tears slid down my father's face, and I felt them well up in my own.

"I miss her too," I whispered.

"You are only eighteen, but you have lived through things which have made you seem older, or more mature to me." He closed his eyes in thought. "I can't imagine what my life would have been like if your mom hadn't said yes to me. Those years with her were the best of my life. She gave me a chance at love." My dad hasn't talked about my mom this much since she died, ever. He looked across the room and past me. I followed his gaze and saw Cooper watching us.

"He loves you," my dad told me.

I smile and would blush if my blood was flowing properly. "I love him too."

"You are going to be fine." He kissed my forehead. "I just wanted you to know that things like life don't always go as planned. Sometimes you just need to work with what is given to you and recognize them as gifts. Ali, you are my gift, and I love you more than anything in the world." The tears were still coming.

"What is it, Dad?" He seemed so distraught as if he was trying to tell me something without giving me any information.

He shrugged. "I just want you to be happy. To be as happy as possible for as long as possible. I don't want you to miss out on anything, because you and I both know how fragile and short life can be."

"I'm happy, Dad," I assured him. He smiled and kissed my hand.

"Get some rest, honey." He stood, resting his hand on the bed.

"I'm not tired." I yawned, and my eyes closed involuntarily. "I just need to rest my eyes for just a minute."

The next time I opened them, almost five hours had passed. I focused on the wall clock then noticed Cooper was sitting next to me with his head on the side of my bed. He was breathing softly, sleeping. I lifted my arm and laid my hand on his head. If I could have moved, I would have kissed him. At least they had exchanged the breathing mask to some of those tubes that stick in your nose. I ran my fingers though Cooper's hair. It looked darker now that he hasn't been in the sun surfing. My fingers ran lightly over his cheek, and the stubble from not shaving for almost two days was showing. Cooper turned his face then sat up.

He blinked a few times, looking at me. "Hey," he said sleepily.

I smiled. "Hey," and he took my hand. "I'm glad you're here, but don't you have to work?" After the words came out, I wished I could take them back. I didn't want him to go anywhere. Cooper made me feel safe, like I was going to make it through this.

"That is one of the things I wanted to talk to you about," he said evenly. I tried to encourage him to continue with my eyes. "I, well . . ." He sounded nervous. "I quit."

What? "You did what?" I didn't understand. "You wanted that job so badly." He took my hands into his and smiled.

"I don't want anything as much as I want you, Ali," he said, and if my heart could beat any harder, you would probably be able to see it though my hospital gown. "I realized that nothing was more important than being with you—nothing."

"But . . . Cooper." I didn't know what to say. He'd given up so much to take this job in the English department. He'd essentially had given up us.

"But nothing," he said, smiling and kissing my hands. "You are my world, Ali. I can't stay away anymore." Cooper shifted in his seat and turned to face me. "There was something else I wanted to talk to you about."

Twelve

Cooper

"What is it, Cooper?" Ali asked me anxiously. "You look upset, so please tell me what is going on." I feel like *my* heart might give out. I swallow and think about the conversation I had with Robert Starr yesterday.

"I didn't know I could feel like this for anyone, Ali. The day I realized I was in love with you, I knew there was only one future for me—you. I have tortured myself staying away from you, and I can't do it anymore, even for just an hour. Your dad and I had a talk about how quickly things can change, and I thought I had almost lost you, more than once. I never want to lose you, Ali. That is why I want to ask you something." I filled my lungs. Ali's beautiful eyes were wide with wonder, and her pale cheeks had a light blush.

"Cooper?" Her voice was hardly audible. I took both her hands in mine.

"I don't ever want to be parted from you, and I need you to fight to stay with me. To know that when you get out of surgery tonight I'll be here waiting for you. I love you so much sometimes I don't know how I lived before I met you. I know that I can't live without you. Allison Marie Starr, will you marry me?" The room went silent, except for Ali's heart monitor. I noticed that the rhythm was faster than it should have been and her breathing was labored. I brushed some loose hair off her face.

"You don't have to answer now. I just had to ask you. I just needed you to know that I am serious about us—as serious as you can get."

"You talked to my dad about this?" she finally asked me.

I nodded slowly. "Yes. I told your dad how much I love you and we talked about the future. I explained to him that I am serious about us being together. I need you to know that when you wake up, I'm not going anywhere." I kiss her hand. "I need you to pull through so you can marry me with your strong heart." I watched as tears welled up in Ali's eyes.

"Cooper," she said, and the tears spilled over, and she looked at our hands. "No." I couldn't tear my eyes away from her face. She silently sobbed, and her thumb traced the back of my hand. Neither of us said anything for a long time. I need to get out of here so I don't break down in front of her. I need to keep a strong disposition. Leave it to me that when I realized this is what I wanted and needed to do, I'd forgotten to take into account that Allison may not want me anymore.

"Fair enough," I managed and swallowed the enormous lump in my throat. I stood and kissed her forehead. "I'm not going anywhere unless you want me to," I said quietly into her skin. She didn't say anything as I left the room.

Trudy and Robert were in the waiting room as I came out. They both stood smiling. I blew past them, unable to even make eye contact. That is not how I saw this going. I made my way to the men's room and locked myself in a stall, leaning against the closed door. No, nothing like this. I let the tears come and rip at the very center of my soul. I guess I had it coming. I had put too much space between us and pushed her away.

I let out a hard cynical laugh. The thing is I do want to marry Ali. I think I knew it on our first date, sharing that first kiss. The thought of losing her is unbearable, but it seems I have lost her. God. What was I thinking? I punch the metal frame of the door before I know what I am doing. Who did I think I was? Blah-blah, I love you. Blah-blah, marry me.

"I am so stupid!" I yell in the empty bathroom. I crumble to the floor, not worrying about germs, and lose it. I am full-on sobbing as I hold my chest, as if it would keep my heart from bursting out. I'm not sure how long I was on the floor, long enough to have stopped crying, but now found myself lost in a maze of emotion. The side of my face is pressed to the door of the cold stall and my arms still wrapped around my chest. I am numb and don't want to feel anything.

"Cooper," a low voice echoed in the tiled room. I didn't answer—I didn't know if I could. A pair of shoes stands outside of my confined pity space. He tries to open the door. "Come on, Cooper, open the door." It's Robert Starr.

"No," I mutter, wondering how long he has been in here. He sighs and tries the door again. "She said no," I say louder. Robert stops trying the door.

"I know, I just talked to her," he told me. "Open the door so we can talk." After a short debate, I turn the silver lock, and he tries to open the door. He pulls me to my feet and is holding me up. I have even lost my will to stand on my own. The way Robert is looking at me makes me want to break down again. Instead I fall into his chest and let him hug me. I have only known him for less than two days, and since that time I told him I am his daughter's teacher—I got punched in the face. I told him I loved his daughter—he understood but wanted to take another swing at me. Then I told him I wanted to marry his only child—he made me explain while he made fists with his hands. I guess I'm lucky for only being punched that one time. I truly should be pummeled for my stupidity.

I explained to him how I felt about Allison. I told him about the most beautiful girl I had ever seen on that beach in San Diego. How when we talked it felt like I had found my home in her. I explained about the mix-up and how I became her teacher and how yesterday I quit my job. I told him I tried to break it off but, by doing so, felt like I was breaking off my arm. I told him that my feelings haven't and wouldn't change. I need her to know that I'm not going anywhere and that she has something to fight for. I know now that it isn't for me, but it needs to be something.

I broke her heart. I am prepared to heal it every single day for the rest of our lives. My only wish is that she would just give me the chance to.

"She doesn't know if she is going to make it—like her mother," Mr. Starr finally said. "She doesn't want to put you through that pain." I turned and held the sink. I had to swallow back the bile that was rising in my throat. I expected him to be relieved that she had turned me down, it was her choice, but he almost looks disappointed. Robert understands and wants a full future for her, no matter how long it may be.

"I just want to make her happy," I tell him. I want to give her as much happiness as possible, I can hardly bear to think what the next part of this, because if she doesn't make it . . . no, she has to make it. I want her to know how much I love her so she can pull through.

"I know my Ali-Oops." Robert clears his throat. "From what I gather over the past seven months, she can't be happy without you either. All she is doing is trying to give you an out, to make you happy."

"That is the most ridiculous, stupid . . ."

"She is doing what she thinks is best, just like you are." His logic is sound.

"Just tell me what to do," I beg him. He shrugs his broad shoulders.

"I can't do that, Cooper. Love is a strange beast." He pats my back sympathetically. "I'm going to go sit with her for a while. Trudy is in there now." He turns to leave me. "They take her in at seven tonight for surgery."

I am alone again. Sometimes I wish for a magic eight ball. Something to give me answers because I just can't trust myself. I know Ali doesn't want to see me, but that doesn't mean I am going to leave. This hospital will be my home until I know that she has made it out of the woods.

Eventually, I leave the restroom. I've been in there so long I must look like a lunatic. I find my way to the waiting room where Trudy tries to comfort me, but I'm beyond comfort. Robert joins us twenty minutes later, and the doctor finds the three of us together and explains what he is going to do in the surgery.

"Allison's aortic vessel needs repair before it can burst. I will open the dilated portion of the aorta and insert a synthetic patch tube. Once the tube is sewn into the aorta, the aneurysmal sac is closed around the artificial tube. Though the surgery is a risk, the risk of rupture is greater." The doctor looks at each of us, expressing the seriousness of the situation. "Allison is a healthy young woman and will be well taken care of." He pauses and speaks only to Robert. "Surgery is a risk, and you must weigh the pros and cons of your options."

Is that supposed to make us feel better? I am going to go slice her freaking heart open and put in a tube. Oh yeah, I am stoked about this. Or if you don't do that, she dies. Just because Ali is a healthy person doesn't mean she is going to be okay. I wish I could trade places with her. I would rip my heart from my chest and give it to her. Now that I think about it, I kind of already did that, and she rejected it.

I watch as Robert and Dr. "Cut-Her-Up" sign some paperwork with a nurse. They both seem calm enough, but I am freaking out over here. I close my eyes and pull Allison's face from the memory of our first date. She flushed often as she answered questions, her smile lighting up my world. Her laugh was contagious and shook me to my core the first time I heard it. Everything about that night was natural, and I had the foolish notion that we would spend many nights like that. Dinner and talking, walking the beach under the stars. Ali was so vibrant and full of life. Now she was defeated and . . .

"Cooper . . ." I look at Mr. Starr. How many times had he said my name before I heard him? I just look up at him. "Allison was asking for you." He puts a hand on my shoulder. "You need to go see her. You'll regret it if you don't."

"Sir." A knot of emotion plagues my nerves. "With all due respect, she doesn't want . . . want me in there," I stammer through the obvious hurt in my words. Robert puts his hands on his hips, and he shakes his head and looks at the ground.

"Go on son." His voice is rough. "She asked me to send you in."

I know what he is saying is true, but I still feel crushed. I make my way to the glass-walled room that Ali is in. I want nothing more than to be with her, help her to not feel scared, but I don't know what I could possibly say or do for her now. I thought I had offered her comfort, but instead I . . . I don't know what I did. I was honest and open, and she swatted me down. Ali made me a better man. I need to keep being that man for her no matter how she may feel about me.

I stand outside her door.

Ali's eyes are closed, and the look on her face is peaceful. I realize that as many times as I have told her that I love her today, she hasn't said it back once. Then why is she asking for me? Is she going to ask me to leave?

Thirteen

Allison

I open my eyes to see that Cooper is standing outside my door. He looks so miserable. For a moment we just stare at each other separated by glass. He looks like he might not come in, so I motion for him to. He hesitates before entering the room, and when he enters, he doesn't come very far inside, and he doesn't look at me. The way he is breathing looks like he is trying to hold himself together. I want him to come to me and hold me close, to kiss my face and tell me everything will be all right.

"Your doctor just explained your procedure," he says, breaking the silence, but won't look at me. I watch him swallow. "Your dad said you asked for me." Not a question, he just wants me to know why he is here.

"Yes," I say, trying to take a deep breath. I am so frustrated at how far from me he is. I want to see into his incredible eyes. "Look at me," I demand, almost yelling it at him. Cooper's head snaps up and is now staring at me; his eyes look like churning water. I can feel the tears burn my own eyes. I raise my hand off the rail and reach for him.

Cooper looks at my hand, and the tears fall onto his cheeks. Slowly, each step taken deliberately, he makes his way to my bedside. He stares at my hand as if it is a foreign object before taking it in his. As soon as our hands touch, I start to relax, but he seems to tense up. What do I say to the guy who just proposed to me? Sorry I said no, that I don't want you to feel the pain of losing me? I can feel the speed of my heartbeat pick up as I realize this might be the last time I see him.

"I know things have changed between us," he says slowly, "but I am going to stick around so I know that you made it out of your surgery all right, just like the doctor said you would." Cooper squeezes my fingers, and a forced smile turns up his lips.

I sigh and close my eyes, forcing my negative thoughts from my mind. "You know why I had to say no," I try to tell him, hoping he understands.

"You need to get your rest." His response is barely audible as he lets my hand go. I open my eyes and watch Cooper take small steps away from me. I want to grab and shake him.

"I just can't," I mumble and start my waterworks. "I can't put you through what my dad went through." Cooper stops and takes a step back toward me.

"*You* are going to make it, Ali," he says in a soothing tone, and I let out a hard laugh.

"Sure I will, just like my mom did." Saying this out loud made me angry. Cooper came back and stood next to me, taking my hand again.

"I know your mom was a great woman, Ali, but you have a different heart. Your heart is stronger." His other hand cupped my face, and warmth filled me. "I understand that I hurt you too much for you to feel the same way toward me, but you are going to go on and live a long happy life." I stared at his soulful blue eyes. I don't understand what he is talking about. Feel the same way toward him? For being such a smart guy, he sure is dense.

"I am trying to let you go on so you can live your life," I try to tell him. What doesn't he understand? Cooper shakes his head.

"I don't think you know how much you mean to me, Allison Starr. Nothing will change how I feel about you. The only way I can go on and live my life is with you." The way he says it sounds like he feels guilty for being so honest.

"Cooper." I want to sit up and put my head against his chest and feel his arms around me.

"I shouldn't have said that." He steps back again. "You need to focus on getting better, not on . . ." He throws his hands up in the air. "I just can't seem to say or do the right thing anymore. I'm sorry." He turns around and is at the door before I could react.

"I love you, Cooper," I blurt out, which uses all my energy. He freezes, as does everything else in my words . "I want to say yes. I want to marry you and make you happy like you make me, but can't you see," I choked out. "Can't you see I just couldn't bear it if I knew you'd be waiting for me and I didn't pull through?"

Without turning around, he answers me. "Can't you see that I want to be there for you when you do pull through? I love you so much that . . ." He doesn't finish his sentence.

"I love you too," I whisper. Saying those three simple words seems to crash into him. When Cooper turns around, his expression is unreadable, but fresh tears cover his cheeks. He moves across the room so quickly it is almost a blur. He takes my head gently in his hands and moves closer as if he is going to kiss me. He pauses just inches from my lips and pulls back. I don't know what expression is on my face, but all I know is how much I love him and hope that is what he sees.

When Cooper's lips finally make contact with mine, nothing else seems to matter to me. I want to wrap my arms around him and pull him closer. He is being so gentle with me as if I am made from glass or a bubble about to pop. I whisper that I love him anytime we parted for air.

Cooper looks at the monitor next to my bedside that is tracking the rhythm of my heart then turns to see the clock on the wall. It is six-thirty. The nurse will be in any second to prep me for surgery and give me a shot to make me groggy, and all I can think about is pulling Cooper into this bed with me. I need to make it out alive for so many reasons, but the only one I can think of now is that I don't want to die a virgin! His fingers touch my cheek lightly and push some loose strands of hair back from my face, and neither of us moves. We just stare at each other, committing the moment to memory.

"I love you," I say quietly. The corners of Cooper's mouth pull up into a crooked smile.

"Ali, I won't make the mistakes of my past anymore." He let out a short puff of air before he continues. "I only wanted what is best for you, and I made all the wrong choices, so you are in control." He looks down at the bed and takes a seat. "I guess what I am trying to say is that the ball is in your court. I will do whatever you want me to do. Whatever will make you happy."

I open my mouth to tell him that *he* is what makes me happy, but I don't because he leans in and kisses my forehead. I hear a noise from behind Cooper, but nothing else matters to me except him knowing how I feel. I slowly lift my hand, which seems to weigh at least fifty pounds, to touch his face. Cooper takes my hand and lifts it the rest of the way for me. My entire body feels heavy and nonfunctional. I want to tell him so many things, but suddenly I am too exhausted to speak, heck, keeping my eyes open is a struggle.

"Cooper," I whisper, at least I think I say his name. He kisses the inside of my palm.

"Yes." His voice is low and hoarse, and he opens my hand so I am cupping his cheek. I sigh and put together my thoughts.

"I do want to marry you," I whisper. "I just wish things were different because I cannot bear to cause you any pain." Now my arms are tingling and my legs are cold. "I want you to go on if I don't make it, okay? I know you'll grieve, but you will also move on." I move my fingers over his face. "You will find a woman who will love you and make you happy, and I want, no, need you to know that I am fine with that." I am surprised Cooper hasn't interrupted me yet, so I continue. "I am just so thankful that I had the chance to fall in love before I meet my maker. You gave me such a precious gift, and I will always be grateful for the summer we spent together." I feel like my head is being lifted up and my body jostled. I force myself to open my eyes.

I am in a hallway, bright lights burning my eyes above me.

Cooper is nowhere around. The nurse had come in and started my prep work when Cooper had sat on my bed. I didn't say any of this monologue out loud; he hadn't heard any of it. I had been being pushed into surgery—drugged—thinking I was giving him permission to let me go. Now he won't know how I feel.

It is too late. I might lose Cooper forever, and he will never know how I truly feel about him. No, this is not happening. I try to push myself up to get my nurse but am unable to do so because the nurse is holding me down, telling me that I need to calm down. I want to scream for her to understand, but it is useless.

No, I plead with my eyes. I need him to know . . . I need him.

Fourteen

Cooper

The last thing Allison said to me was my name. It looked like she wanted to say more, but then those stupid drugs took her straight to la-la land. At least she looked peaceful and relaxed. I did kiss her soft lips one last time before they wheeled her out. Now I have to sit here for who knows how long, praying I get to hear the end of her sentence. Just so I can see her one last time, even if it is to tell me to kick rocks and leave her alone. At least if she is telling me to get lost, that means she made it through and is alive.

I thought of how fragile she felt under my touch. Is she really strong enough to make it through such a tough surgery?

No, Cooper. You can't think like that, my brain tells me. I close my eyes and scoot down in my chair, propping my head on my hands and elbows on my knees. This can't be real. I am having a nightmare, and when I wake up, Ali will be just fine. Maybe I fell asleep on the beach and we are still in San Diego at the water's edge, the hot sun covering our bodies and the cold waves slithering up the sand to our feet.

"I am going to the cafeteria. Would you like some coffee?" I look up, and Trudy is talking to me. I hope I am not dreaming about Trudy now. She shakes my shoulder, and I realize I am just staring at her— awake—not dreaming.

"Uh, no, thank you," I tell her as I try to focus on the here and now. She shrugs and takes in a deep breath.

"You got to think positive, Ryan. Ali is going to pull through. I just know she will." I want to laugh and cry. I haven't slept in almost two days, and I think I am starting to lose my grip on reality.

"You know what, you are right." I stand up, and Trudy's eyes go wide at my sudden movement. "Coffee would be nice too." I try to smile, but I'm sure it looks like a grimace. I pull out my wallet and hand her some money then sit back down. I look at my watch to see how long they have had Ali back there; it seems like it has been hours. I am shocked to see it has only been about twenty minutes. Mr. Starr is sitting a few chairs down from me, head bowed in silent prayer.

I wish I could think of something to say to him, to both of us, to make this easier. Nothing can be said to make this any less hard on us. I put my head back in my hands and let my eyes close. It's not like I am going to be able to sleep, not until I know she is okay; my eyes are just so heavy. I take some slow deep breaths and know that if I weren't so worried, I could fall asleep in a matter of minutes. I can hear someone walking toward me and look up, expecting Trudy with my coffee.

It is a nurse dressed in all-blue surgical scrubs, and she looks upset. Mr. Starr and I jump to our feet in synchronization, thinking the same thing—this can't be good news. The nurse looks back and forth between the two of us then lands her gaze on me.

"Cooper," she says, sounding frustrated. Her brown hair is tucked neatly in a scrub cap, and a name badge is clipped to the hem of her top which has her picture and name printed on the plastic—Laura.

"Yes," I mumble. She waves her hand in a motion to follow her and takes a step away.

"Allison won't let us start on her until she can talk to you," Laura says loud enough for Robert to hear. "She is agitated and upset, so maybe you can help calm her down." I nod and follow her behind doors labeled Restricted. "I need you to come in here first." We stop in front of a door which leads into a room lined with stainless steel sinks.

I follow her lead and scrub all the way up to my elbows for what seems like an hour. Out of nowhere another nurse appears and dries my hands and arms then slides them into some latex gloves. When they are on, she slips a mask over my face and then is gone. I am just standing there feeling like I am in a hidden-camera show, not knowing what to do.

"This way," Laura says as she uses her back to open yet another set of doors. Of course I follow her not knowing what I'll see behind these doors.

I wasn't prepared for what happened next.

I'm standing in a surgical bay, Ali's surgical bay to be exact. Ali is in a bed with straps across her body, and tubes are sticking out from all over. Huge bright lights are on overhead, and monitors beep in compulsive intervals. Then I noticed everyone else: Ali's doctor next to a tray of shiny tools and about ten other nurses, not including the one who had come to get me, and maybe two more doctors. Laura led me forward gently with her gloved hand on my back.

Ali's eyes were closed and her breathing steady. "Here is Cooper for you, Allison," Laura said slowly. Her eyes opened, and she searched the room. I moved to be in her view, which meant stooping next the operating table.

"Cooper," Ali whispered and smiled. I couldn't help but to smile back and felt tears burn at my eyes. "They gave me drugs," she mused. This statement got a few snickers from the audience, which I ignored. I wanted to scoop her into my arms and take her far from here, to protect her.

I touched her head with my glove-covered hand and smiled. "Allison, they need to start so they can fix you up," I told her softly, trying to soothe her. Ali rolled her eyes.

"I know . . . I know," she said sleepily as her eyes closed again. "But I wanted to . . . to tell you something . . . important . . . and I thought I had . . . but . . . shot . . . then I realized I hadn't," she babbled. I nodded, pretending to understand what she meant.

"What is it?" I asked, suddenly wishing we weren't surrounded by all these people. What if she wanted to tell me she didn't want me here when she wakes up? I think my heart would need a doctor.

"I was going to . . . to tell you to move on . . . if I don't make it." She looked me straight in the eyes. "That you will be able to find someone . . ."

"Ali," I whispered and moved closer, our faces inches apart, and touched her lips with my gloved finger.

"Lemme finish," she gurgled. "Then I wanted to tell you . . . no . . . to thank you for giving me the best summer of my life." I couldn't stop the tears. "That you gave me the greatest gift when . . . when you gave me your love. So then I thought . . . hey . . . you are mine . . . so . . . I don't want you to find someone else," she slurred, sounding almost drunk. I watched her carefully, and she looked like she knew what she was saying. Her dark brown eyes were lucid, and she smiled.

"Okay," I said through my mask, the one on my face and the metaphoric one holding back my emotions. "I won't."

Ali smirked. "Ask me again." I shook my head, confused. "Ask me, Cooper." Her voice was low and raspy. I took a deep breath, trying to process what she was saying. I'd asked her if she wanted me to leave, but she hasn't sent me away. She just told me she didn't want me to find someone else, but she had declined me. *Ask me again*, she had said. I looked into her waiting eyes and arched an eyebrow. Was she serious?

What the hell—you only live once, right? Bad timing on that thought.

"Allison Starr," I spoke quietly just to her, blocking out all the other people in the room. "I promise to heal your heart every single day for the rest of our lives." I took a deep breath. "Will you marry me?" Tears streamed from the dark pools of Allison's eyes.

"Yes," she whispered, and I noticed there wasn't a dry eye in operation bay 2. "I was being so stupid before," she said loudly. "Yes, Cooper. I will marry you." My heart pumped so hard in my chest I was sure it was going to explode. I wanted to kiss her, but this stupid mask was in the way.

"Yes," I repeated back, unsure. "You want to marry me?" She tried to nod, but her head had a strap across it.

"I wanted to save you from this, well, from me, but I just love you too much, and like my dad said, 'life is too short,' so yes," Ali said easily. I couldn't help it, I leaned over and kissed her through my mask.

"You are going to marry me?" I asked again, shocked. Ali laughed, and it sounded better than any sound I had ever heard. "You better be sure because I have witnesses." I motioned to the room with my eyes.

"Well, you better be sure because they are going to fix me up and hold you to it," she joked. I leaned in as close as I could get to her ear.

"I have been sure since the first day I saw you," I said so only she could hear. "I love you." I touched my forehead to hers. I unwillingly stood up to leave. Nurse Laura, who had retrieved me, had to return me. Her eyes were red with emotion. Before I left, I turned back to the room.

"That's my fiancée," I almost yelled with a smile. The medical staff laughed and then got to work. The nurse had me scrub up to my elbows again.

"That was the most romantic thing I have ever seen," Laura said, not looking at me. "And you both are so young," she continued, "but so sure." She is right, I am sure.

I found myself back in the waiting room but did not remember how I walked back. Allison had said yes to me—to marry me. Trudy was standing with Mr. Starr holding two cups of coffee. Their conversation stopped when they saw me, looks of concern covering their faces. I don't know what I looked like, but for as happy as I felt, I'm sure I looked terrified.

"Cooper," Robert said, frantic. "What is it?" I stood arm's length from him as I gathered my thoughts. I was just going to blurt it out but then thought better of it. I mean, come on, the last thing I wanted was to be punched out again just from pure surprise.

I looked up into his face then closed my eyes. "She said yes," I spoke carefully and slowly, letting the shock of the reality sink into my body. The silence made me open my eyes so I could see his expression. Mr. Starr nodded in thought and looked toward Trudy who nodded as well, as if they had a silent conversation in which they agreed upon something.

"Then she will fight to survive," Robert finally said, gripping my shoulder in his hand. "You gave her your heart, son, and now she will fight to keep it beating."

His words shook me to my core. They held so much meaning and truth. I hadn't noticed Trudy was crying. Mr. Starr, or my soon-to-be father-in-law, pulled me into a bear of an embrace. I hugged him back, knowing we both understood each other more than we ever thought could be possible. Ali had said yes. She did love me the same as I loved her.

Forever.

Forever would be the easy part. The now is the hard part—the waiting—waiting to hear that the love of my life was going to make it through one of the most difficult surgeries. But that is all I can do, wait. So wait I will.

***

Seven hours is a long time to try not to worry. I did sleep for a couple of hours, not well, but it was something. When I woke up, the waiting room was filled with students from Chino Prep. I recognized most of them. The two that stood out were Jeremy and Christina. Jeremy was giving me the death stare, and Christina, well, she looked like she understood. Had Allison told her about us? It didn't matter anymore. I was no longer their teacher. I closed my eyes and leaned my head back against the wall, trying to forget about the dozens of eyes that kept glancing in my direction.

I hadn't realized I dozed off again, but when my eyes snapped open, another hour had passed.

"There is still no update," a voice said from next to me. I turned and was surprised to find Christina next to me. Jeremy was still across the room sitting with a small cluster of friends, some crying and some holding on to each other for support.

"Uh, thanks," I stuttered. Christina smiled faintly, and I felt a little awkward.

She let out a long sigh and leaned her head closer to me. "Ali told me you dumped her as soon as you found out you'd be her teacher," she stated. I didn't know how I should respond, but I didn't have to because she continued. "I knew she wasn't over you, and then over winter break she was alive again. It was like she didn't know how to be happy without you, and you gave her joy again."

I turned to face Christina straight on. "I never stopped loving her," I whispered. She smiled and nodded. I had never talked to Christina before; she wasn't one of my students. She was average height, about 5'4", and her shoulder-length blonde hair curled at the ends. She had dark green eyes, the color of emeralds, and a cute round face to set off her perky nose. Christina has a soothing voice filled with reason. There is no judgment in her; she seems loyal and compassionate.

"What are you going to do?" Her questioning was intense and almost as painful as my black eye.

"Well, between us." I waited as she nodded again. "I quit Chino Prep and asked Allison to marry me."

Christina's well-guarded face turned into a mask of shock. She glanced over to Mr. Starr. "Does he know?" Her voice was low and almost harsh.

I almost laughed. "Of course he does." I pointed to my swollen eye. "Robert knows everything about Ali and me." *Well, as much as a father should know,* I amended in my head. Christina was quiet in thought before she spoke again.

"Well, did she say yes?" Ali's best friend finally asked. I smiled for the first time in hours.

"Would you like to hear the story?" She nodded as I proceeded to tell her the story, not just the proposal—all of it. The first time I saw Allison on the beach, our first meeting and kiss. I explained the school mix-up and the agony I had been in ever since. When I finished, Christina's eyes were filled with tears, and she hugged me quickly.

"It's all so . . . incredible," she said, her voice hardly audible, emerald eyes sparkling with tears. "I just can't believe what you both have been through."

"Me neither," I admitted. We both sat silently, processing the weight of the circumstance that still lies ahead. Christina took my hand and squeezed it in hers.

"Allison is the strongest and bravest person I have ever met," she tells me but doesn't look at me. "I won't tell anyone what you shared with me, but I think the rumors will be hard on Ali, though she would never let on that it bothers her."

"Rumors . . ."

"Look, Mr. Perez, we are all in high school, and there are people that are here wondering what you are doing *here*. The gossip is bound to fly." The truth of her words stings in the open wound of my heart. Would poor Ali never have a break?

"Well," I start to say but have to stop to swallow the lump in my throat. "You can tell them that I found her and rode with her to the hospital. You can also inform your classmates that I am no longer their teacher and, Christina." She looks up at me with innocent round eyes. "Please call me Cooper or Coop." Christina laughs, which seems like a forbidden sound in the waiting room.

"I can see why Ali fell so hard for you . . . Cooper. And I'll keep the sharks at bay." With that, my new ally crosses the ocean of bloodthirsty predators to defend myself and the woman I love. I lean my head to rest

165

against the wall, and my eyes slowly droop. Before they close, two more people enter the waiting room, but my eyes are too heavy to identify them.

"Cooper," the woman says. *That woman sounds like my mom,* I muse. "Cooper, honey," she says and touches my arm. I force my eyelids open and look at the lady next to me.

"Mom?" My foggy brain is trying to compute. "How did . . . when . . . who . . . ?" I didn't know where to start. I was trying to ask how she knew where I was, when did she get here, and who told her what was going on. Then I noticed the other person that was with her, Sean. He looked so subdued, which wasn't fitting for him, even under the circumstances.

"Trudy called the restaurant looking for me. She told me what was going on and that you could use a friend," Sean explained, and then a small smile crossed his lips. "It looks like you could have used backup. What happened to your face?" My mom touched the tender skin around my eye, and I winced back in pain.

"That would be me," Mr. Starr spoke up. "There was uh . . . a misunderstanding."

"You are Ali's dad then, huh?" Sean asked, fairly amused.

"Sure am, Robert Starr." The tall muscular man stuck out his hand and shook Sean's in return. My mother stood up and was so petite she looked half his size. Knowing my mom, she'd probably try to punch Robert for what he'd done to my face—an eye for an eye.

"Hello, I am Danielle Perez," she said calmly as she took her turn shaking Mr. Starr's hand. I jumped up before anyone else could talk.

"Uh, Mom . . . I need to talk to you," I blurted out. They both looked at me as if I was a lunatic. She dropped his hand and looked at me quizzically.

"Sure, son," she said slowly and suspiciously before she turned back to Robert. "And you and I will talk later about that black eye you gave my boy." I covered my face with my hands, but to my surprise, Mr. Starr was laughing.

"I'll let him explain." He paused as I looked at him. "Everything." The weight of *everything* was almost too much to bear. Sean took a step toward me, looking as uncomfortable as anyone would after two hours in the car with my mom.

"Hey, man." I pull him in by the shoulder. "Thanks for coming." His arms flash around me and tighten.

"I'm not here for you." His words are almost comical. I lean back to see what he means. "Book Girl is going to need someone to hold her when she wakes up, and who is to say she won't be asking for me?" The sound that escapes my throat is a cross between a laugh and a sob. Should I just ask him to be my best man so he gets the idea? Nah, I need to see the shock on his face when the time is right.

I turn toward the group of students still huddled in the corner. "Christina," I call just loud enough. Her eyes snap to mine as she stands and crosses the room. When she reaches Sean and me, she stands silently at my side. "Sean, this is Allison's best friend, Christina . . . Christina, this is my best friend, Sean." They both reach out to shake hands.

"Nice to meet you," Sean says, very debonair. I half expected him to bow and kiss her hand.

"And you, Sean," Christina says, just as charmed. I look back between the two of them; they are still in a handshake that—let's face it—is now just handholding.

I clear my throat. "Christina, would you mind filling Sean in on all the details." I lean in to whisper in her ear. "Except the proposal, I need to tell him that myself." Christina nods and smiles.

"Come on," Sean protests. "Since when do you keep secrets from me?" I open my mouth to explain but find Christina handling it.

"Since you lost privileges by getting here so late," she snaps in an adorably playful way. I've never seen Sean swoon, but I'm pretty sure this is what it looks like on him. I watch them walk off together and know I left them each in the right hands. I knew Sean would like Christina; she is a pretty blonde and feisty.

My mom and I excused ourselves, and we didn't make it far before my mom turned and without words demanded answers. First, I had to give her the questions that she didn't know to ask. We found a deserted corridor and took seats next to each other.

"Son." She touched my cheek. "First, are you doing okay?" I looked into her eyes, which was like looking into mine. This is my mom, the woman who would bring me a drink when I was sick with a straw bent in a crazy direction to cheer me up, who would patch up all my scraps and wounds, the woman who taught me how to love and be loved in return. She is my safety net.

"Mom"—my throat tightened—"she can't die." I watched her eyes fill with tears as she swallowed. My mom had spent some time with Ali this summer and fell just as much in love as I did. They had spent hours talking, and my mom taught Ali how to cook some of our family's traditional dishes. My mom knew the pain it had caused me to have to end things with her. I think it hurt her almost as much.

Mom took my hand in hers. "So why don't you start explaining everything . . . starting with the black eye." I let out a humorless laugh and told her about meeting Robert Starr for the first time. I tried to play the victim, but my mom said she had to forgive him because of the shock.

"He didn't know?" Her hand covered her mouth in a ladylike fashion.

"I guess not, but he figured it out pretty fast." My mom looked into my eyes for a moment.

"When I spoke to you at Christmas, I asked if you had seen Ali, and you told me no. That you needed to stay in town to work on lesson plans." Over the phone I could hide more from my mom, but in person she extracted the truth like a mind reader.

"I couldn't help it." I sounded like a pouty four-year-old. She just shook her head.

"The way you two are together is like . . . bread and butter. It would be unnatural to be apart." My mouth dropped open. This is why we have mothers, they just make everything right sometimes. I put my head on her shoulder, craving the comfort I have needed the last two days.

"Now," she said quietly, "tell me about quitting your job." I sat up robotically and just stared at her calm face. "I'm no fool, son. You didn't think that John wouldn't call me." It wasn't a question. I should have realized that the first thing John would do is call my mom. Never trust a lawyer.

I wanted to deny or explain. Instead I found myself saying something completely different. "I didn't have a choice." I anticipated her telling me that I always had a choice. Wrong.

"There will be another job." I'd always known my mom to be understanding, but this was . . . unreal. Maybe she knew how I was plagued with anxiety right now and was staying calm for my benefit. That just made me love her more.

So I guess I'll test my theory. "I asked her to marry me." Now my mom looked at me shocked. "She said yes . . . so . . . you'll be getting that daughter you always wanted." Big tears rolled delicately from my mom's eyes. "Are those happy tears?" I finally asked as I pulled her in for a hug.

It took her a moment to answer. "Yes," she said in a gasp of breath. She hugged me back hard, and we both cried in earnest. There was a silver lining on the dark cloud that hung over the circumstances, but at least we had that. Hope and love.

Mom and I eventually went back to the waiting room to rejoin our group. Mr. Starr's eyes had been closed until my mom walked up to him, hands on her hips. He jumped to his feet, expecting a mother's revenge, but he didn't know my mom. Dwarfed in comparison, my five-foot-tall mom wrapped her arms around Robert and just held him. For a moment, he was too dazed to respond but then tentatively returned the gesture. They just stood there . . . holding each other in some sort of parental understanding. I took my seat and continued with the waiting game.

The hours seemed to continue to drag on, every minute taking an hour. At the seven-hour mark, the doctor had sent a nurse to inform us the procedure will be longer than he had first expected. It was Laura, and she told us that it could be two, maybe three, more hours before they were finished. Of course we all had questions, and all she could tell us was that Ali was stable. The way she said stable sounded unsure, which led to a different round of questions.

Laura held up her hands in a surrender position. "Look, if I had more information, I would be happy to give it to you. I need to get back in there." She left before we could ask another thing. I looked around the almost-empty waiting room. All of Allison's classmates had left except for Christina who was sitting with Sean. I sat alone and watched as Trudy, Mom, and Robert all whispered close together. Sean had an arm around Christina, letting her head rest on his shoulder, and she held the hand that stretched across his lap. Lonely doesn't seem like a strong-enough word for how I am feeling. I let my head rest against the back wall and replayed every second I had with Ali over and over in my mind.

Four hours later, Allison's doctor emerged from the "restricted" doors. His face was ashen and drawn. He stood before our group which consisted of me, Robert, Trudy, Mom, Sean, and Christina. The doctor cleared his throat and wiped the back of his hand over his forehead before he spoke. He looked from Mr. Starr then to me then closed his eyes and shook his head in shock.

"Mr. Starr," the doctor's tired voice croaked, "this type of procedure is very difficult . . ." Robert's arm wrapped around my shoulder as my legs started to give way. I knew Ali's dad was crying, and I could feel tears rolling down my own cheeks. Everyone around us started to hold one another in support. Sean's arms supported both Trudy and Christina while my mom's arm was around my waist and holding Mr. Starr's free hand; Trudy put an arm around my mom which connected us all. The doctor continued.

"Allison's heart . . . well . . . her heart . . . stopped beating for over two minutes when we took her off bypass." He had to pause at our sounds of despair. "We tried everything that we *medically* could, but we just couldn't . . ." I stopped listening. Sound no longer reached my eardrums. Every part of me trembled with disbelief. No. No, there had to be some kind of mistake. If I could only go back there and see her—I'm sure she is going to be fine. She has to be fine.

I was vaguely aware that the doctor was still talking, but I still wasn't hearing.

"Let me see her," I demanded loudly. The doctor blinked a few times, and his eyes opened wide.

"I don't think that's a good idea right now . . ."

"I said LET ME SEE HER NOW!" I yelled. Robert gripped my shoulders, and Sean put a hand on my chest. I shook them both off.

"Coop, listen, the doctor was just saying . . . ," Sean started telling me until I shot him a look. He stopped midsentence but left his hand on my shoulder.

I was breathing hard and fast, hoping I wouldn't pass out or throw up. The doctor stared at me for a full minute before he responded to my yelling fit. The group around me seemed almost calm, which just amped me up even more. They must be in shock, that is the only reasonable response for why they have the frozen look of disbelief on their faces. I looked at the doctor who seemed to be avoiding my eye contact. He looked to Robert's shocked face who just nodded.

"Very well," the doctor said briskly.

I turned to look at the group of people who all loved Allison. I nodded once then followed the doctor back though the "restricted" doors like I had a very long eleven hours ago. I didn't know what to expect or where the doctor was taking me. I could feel my hands shaking and my heart thumping in my chest. We stopped at the end of the hallway. This is it. I swallowed the huge lump in my throat and blinked back the tears burning in my eyes.

I looked at the doctor then toward the closed door. The doctor eyed me suspiciously. I know that he is probably waiting for the tough guy who yelled at him in front of a group of people. I'm not that guy right now. I am broken and unraveled. The other half that had made me whole is . . .

I took a deep breath and pushed the door open with my trembling hands. I headed for the curtained-off area which was surrounded by nurses. Every step I took felt like I was walking the plank or down death row. One more step and it might be my last. The nurse who had brought me back to Allison all those hours ago saw me walking toward her and met me halfway.

"Cooper," Laura said, "how did you get back here?" Her voice was soft and calm—placating.

"The doctor," I managed to croak out. She touched my arm, and I couldn't look her in the eyes. There was some movement, and it took me a moment to see that I was now alone. Ha, what an understatement. I reached for the curtain, and two torturous minutes later, I willed myself to pull it back to see my Ali, or . . . what was left of her.

I heard the cry leave my throat, and there was no stopping the tears from my eyes. I felt faint and shaky knowing all the blood just rushed from my body. I took a step closer. I didn't know what I should have expected when I first walked through those doors, but I never would have thought to expect this. I was stunned knowing my life would never be the same.

That was my last thought before I passed out.

Fifteen

Robert

Two years later

Twelve years ago I had to do the unthinkable, bury the woman that I loved. Though the pain was almost unbearable, I never knew that I would suffer something even more excruciating—watch my only child endure the same disease. As a father, you would do anything for your baby, but I was unable to give my daughter my heart. At eighteen, Allison suffered from an aortic aneurysm. If it hadn't been for her teacher at the time, Cooper Perez, she wouldn't have even made it to the hospital, let alone surgery.

That was also the day I discovered that the boy Ali had met at the beach over her summer break, Cooper, was one and the same. After I punched the guy in the face, my sister, Trudy, explained everything to me. It's not that I liked the situation, but I respected the guy. He was willing to stand up to me because of how much he loved my daughter. Not only stand up to me, but quit his job to stay by her side. The guy is a ten in my book. That's why I could understand when he told me he wanted to ask Ali to marry him. He couldn't stand being without her for another minute.

I would give anything for another minute with Allison's mom. After Cooper and I talked about it for almost an hour, he had my blessing. Life could be over in the blink of an eye, so we need to take advantage of every second God gives to us. It was devastating watching Cooper's heartbreak as Ali told him no. I understand why she thought she was doing the right thing, but she was also only hurting herself. I'd like to say I was surprised when she changed her mind and demanded the nurse bring Cooper to the operating table, but I wasn't. He asked again, and she said yes.

Then we had to wait through a seven-hour surgery that took over eleven hours due to complications. I'll never forget the look on the doctor's face as he made that long walk into the waiting room. His expression said it all before he even explained. I replay his words often like he said them yesterday.

"Mr. Starr," his voice low and echoing back to me from memory, "this type of procedure is difficult . . ." Allison's heart had completely stopped, and it took them two long minutes before it would start again. It was a battle from there on out. I remember putting my arm around Cooper, thinking he was close to fainting, as close as I was. Tears flowed wildly down both our faces as we listened to the rest. At that moment, Cooper and I had a bond that could never be broken.

Two men—two women—four broken hearts.

I am waiting inside a church for Cooper now. It's a beautiful spring afternoon. I glance at my watch just as he comes through the door. He smiles, and all the pain and worry from the past is absent.

"I'm not late." He laughs as he approaches me for a hug.

"I never said you were, son." I pat his back and smile. Cooper is dressed in a black suit which makes his blue eyes even brighter. "Are you ready for this?" I ask him.

He lets out a long breath of air and smiles bigger. "I sure am." His answer is as sure as the sunrise.

"I'll be right back." I nod and pat his shoulder. "Wait here."

I never thought two years ago that this is where we all would end up, but I couldn't be any happier than I am right now. I knock lightly on the door in the back of the church. Christina cracks the door open, her eyes bright and as green as grass.

"Is it time?" she asked, grinning as she pushed open the door just enough for me to squeeze through.

"It is," I stated as I entered the tiny room and felt my throat constrict.

Inside was a flurry of pale yellow, dusty pinks, and a variety of flowers. I took two careful steps toward the billowing white waterfall in the center of it all. Her dark hair was up, and small curls trickled throughout. Her cheeks burned pink with excitement and dark chocolate brown eyes wide and shining. Her smile covered her face as she stood to face me.

"Are you ready to give me away, Daddy?" Allison asked softly. I swallowed hard as I took her delicate hands in mine.

"Never," I whispered with a smile.

Two years ago the doctor told Cooper and me that this kind of procedure is difficult, but he added not impossible. Allison's heart *had* stopped for two whole minutes, and nothing seemed to work to revive her. Then the nurse who had brought Cooper back into to the operating room, Laura, before Ali went under tried something different.

"That boy is out there waiting to marry you, Allison Starr," she said loudly into Ali's ear. "So don't you let him down. You keep fighting." The entire operating room had gone silent in shock at what Laura had just done. So silent that the only sound you could hear was the increasing rate of Ali's now-beating heart. It took a moment for the medical staff to spring back into action after watching what they later would describe as a medical miracle.

Cooper had truly given Allison his heart all right and all the love it carried. His love for my baby girl saved her that day. Looking back, it was like his heartbeat traveled through the halls and straight into hers and just . . . well, it was like he was beating for the both of them. That day when the doctor came to give us the news, Cooper told me he hadn't heard a thing he said; he just knew that he had to see her. I can only imagine his surprise when he pulled back the recovery room curtain to find her alive. Not just alive but awake.

When he woke back up from his fainting spell, they didn't see any harm letting him recover in the bed next to Ali's. She had to stay in the hospital for a couple of weeks and then was declared with a clean bill of health. She couldn't go back to school right away, but she had a supportive tutor who gave as much time as she needed, Cooper. I all but let him move in with us. When Ali felt up to it, I let him take her to dinner, knowing what he was up to. That night she came home with a permanent smile and a two-karat diamond engagement ring. That is the night I made Cooper move out; no need to create temptation. Allison graduated that summer, just as planned.

The church is filled with over two hundred people who have touched Cooper's and Allison's lives in some way or another—the doctors who worked to seal up the hole in her heart, the nurse who made her keep fighting, and so many friends and family who were just as anxious to see Ali pull through as Cooper and I were. I take Ali's arm and loop it through mine. Her ivory lacy wedding dress cuts straight across her chest and shows almost an inch of her healed incision. She chose not to cover it completely saying that it is a visible reminder of what love can do.

Together, Ali and I stand at the back of the church waiting for the music to start. On our cue, we make our way down a petal-covered aisle. The entire church stands to see the beautiful bride make her journey toward the groom. Cooper's blue eyes are wide, and his smile says it all as he watches my little girl make her way toward him. A thousand memories flash in my mind: Allison taking her first steps, learning to ride a bike, her eyes on Christmas morning. None of those happy memories can compare to right now. My baby made it though her surgery and has a long healthy life ahead of her. We reach the front of the church, and I place Ali's hand in Cooper's. Allison turns to kiss me on the cheek.

"I love you, Daddy," she whispers in my ear.

"I love you, baby girl," I whisper back. Cooper shakes my hand and secures my gaze in his. I know how much he loves her, and he will stop at nothing to make her happy.

I walked my little Ali-Oops down the aisle today. I gave her away to the only man I trust with her heart. The man who saved my baby with the only thing that could—unconditional love.

Life will throw a lot at you, so you can count on learning something new every day. I have learned to open my heart and let life teach me whatever it has to offer. Every day is a gift wrapped in the lessons of tomorrow.

Today, life has taught me there is a happily ever after.

Teach Me

Special Thanks and Acknowledgements

There are so many people that make writing possible.

First, my true love and high school sweetheart, Joel. Thank you for always supporting me and giving me inspiration it takes to persist. You are the greatest man in the world and I constantly in awe of how much I love you. Second, my mom. Mom, this story specifically makes me think of you. The day I tried to explain it to you and couldn't see how it could work out. And the day you read the first draft and called me in tears because you loved everything about it! Thank you for being my constant cheerleader and encouraging me even when you don't know how it's going to end.

My Red Pen club. You all are so amazing for being willing to read and re-read my drafts. There are not enough words to express my gratitude. Andrea Harris-Estes, Cori Ciocon, Caitlyn Decker and Melissa Stahly. Thank you for all your kindness and encouragement. Thank you for always being willing to let me ramble about people who don't exist outside my brain and not having me committed. You are all the picture of what true friendship looks like.

Thank you to Laura Kerns for your professional insight. I appreciate that you took the time to make my sterile medical jargon into a proper conversation. Thank you for your time and help, it's greatly appreciated. Creative liberties were made and I apologize if any of the information isn't 100% kosher.

Writing is truly a passion for me. This story is particularly holds a special place in my heart.

In the words of Oscar Wilde "Men always want to be a woman's first love—Women like to be a man's last romance." I wanted to write a story to make both true and real.

Made in the USA
San Bernardino, CA
08 December 2013